THE
BROKEN BOW

THE BROKEN BOW

Pauline Thompson

Christian Focus Publications

ISBN 1 871 676 98 3

Published by
Christian Focus Publications Ltd
Geanies House, Fearn, Ross-shire,
IV20 1TW, Scotland, Great Britain.

Cover design
by
Seoris N. McGillivray

Printed and bound in Great Britain by
Cox & Wyman Ltd, Reading, Berkshire

CONTENTS

1

A THIEF!

Sunlight was filtering through the trees that huddled together on the mountain side. The undergrowth was dense, and you or I would not have noticed the brown-skinned boy, a bunch of leaves covering his buttocks, who slipped silently down to the river. Someone had seen him however, for a call rang out from the hill beyond.

'Kisoo-oo-oo-oo!'

Kisoo ignored it, choosing instead to search for the good drinking water which would satisfy his thirst. He soon found the pipe-shaped leaf marking the spot where water gushed from the river bank, and drank thirstily. Then he filled the gourd he had been carrying, sealed it with some leaves and stood it carefully behind a rock. Not until then did he answer the call. 'Yoo-oo-oo!' He cupped his hands above his head, as if this would help to send his voice ringing up the mountain side.

The conversation continued, singing to and fro in

ringing tones as Kisoo made his way up towards the unseen friend.

'Come - oo!'

'I am coming - oo!'

'From where are you coming?'

They had met now, and sought out a clearing in the sun, for the air was still chill. Weapons were laid aside, and Kisoo took acorns out of his net bag, preparing for a game of marbles.

The boys were of short, stocky build and about twelve years old, though they would not have known it. They measured their age by dry seasons, which were not always regular. Kisoo and Aipi had the same father but different mothers, and did not often see each other. To have several wives was economy for the highlanders, for that was to have more than one garden, more pigs, and of course many children. Kisoo's father had four wives, and was known as a rich man.

'Have you been hunting?' Kisoo asked.

'No, no,' was the response, 'but one never knows. I wouldn't like to meet a wild pig and be unprepared.'

'I was helping my mother with the garden,' Kisoo volunteered, as they spun the acorns. 'But that is women's work!' He spat. 'So I said I would come to fetch her water to drink.'

Again they became absorbed in their game, until

Kisoo could see that he was losing.

'My mother will be angry. I must go.'

Aipi laughed. 'She'll only throw her digging stick at you. You can jump out of the way.' He was searching for a way to keep him a little longer.

'I know where we can find possum,' he volunteered.

'Where?' Kisoo asked, his mother and her anger forgotten.

'I'm not telling you,' he tantalised. 'But - I'll show you. We'll go together, just you and I, without the others. It is time we showed them that we can hunt.'

The brothers made their plan. They would wait until the next moonlit night and meet at the river crossing that lay half-way between their homes.

'I am going,' Kisoo announced.

'You go.'

The boys gathered up their acorns and weapons and slipped away in their different directions.

Two days passed before the rain cleared. 'There will be a moon tonight,' Kisoo whispered to himself. 'We'll go hunting for possum.'

As darkness fell, the women gathered the pigs and smaller children into their houses. Kisoo crouched to make his way in through the low porchway of the man house.

His father had already come, but there was

another wig and a bow left there, which he did not recognise. Sure enough, squatting with his father beside the fire, was a stranger.

'Who is he?' Kisoo whispered to his brother. He knew they must not interrupt the man talk.

'He is father's cousin, Ayak, come from the other side of the blue mountain. He has been looking for a pig that was lost. Father met him up the mountain and brought him to stay for the night.'

The stranger took out a parcel of leaves from his net bag and unwrapped some skinny frogs. Tying them on to a stick, he hung them over the fire to roast.

'These will make a tasty morsel to add to our sweet potato,' he told them. 'I caught them by the river.'

Having the stranger with them was a good reason for spending a long time around the fire exchanging folk tales. The highland people excelled in telling stories, and as a good one was judged by its length, it was a long time before the men retired to their wooden beds.

Then the boys covered the glowing embers of the fire with ash, burying in it the sweet potato that would be their meal for the next day.

Kisoo, lying beside the warm hearth, struggled to keep awake. It seemed a very long time before the restless movements had ceased and snores were rising and falling like the roar of a distant waterfall. Silently he got to his knees and crept towards the doorway. In the porch he slipped an axe into his belt. He did not bother with the bunch of leaves worn as clothing, but reached instead to pick up his bow.

Kisoo paused. Lying beside his own bow was that of the stranger. It was strong and supple and made from a different wood. If it had belonged to someone of his own clan it wouldn't have mattered, but of course he could not take that of an outsider. Yet still he hesitated. Wouldn't that add to the excitement? After all, it wasn't stealing, but being found out that was a disgrace. And he would put it back before anyone was awake.

Kisoo was nervous as he ran along the path and down through the trees towards the river. Surely the spirits would not be abroad in the moonlight, for they were of the darkness. Even so, he started at every shadow and paused nervously on approaching the rocks where they had agreed to meet. Suddenly, he gave a stifled scream as something leapt out of the darkness.

'Hush, you fool,' whispered Aipi, his hand covering Kisoo's mouth. 'You'll frighten all the possum for miles around.'

The two boys disappeared deep into the forest. They came to a sturdy oak that stood guardian among the smaller trees and helped each other to climb into its branches. 'We are sure to see one from here,' they affirmed.

Hours seemed to pass as the boys waited in tense silence, their eyes searching the darkness.

Suddenly, with a loud beating of wings, an owl brushed past the branch where they were sitting. Kisoo started with fright, almost losing his balance. A commotion of scurrying began in the bushes below. The two, with hearts beating rapidly, set their bows at the ready. Silence. The offender was only a rat and Aipi signalled to let it go. They were hoping for bigger game.

Kisoo opened his eyes with a start. He must have fallen asleep, for Aipi was tapping him with his bow and pointing to the sky. 'It's too late now,' he whispered,' we'd better go back.'

Weary with cold and disappointment, the brothers clambered stiffly down the tree. Kisoo was anxious to return the bow before the stranger woke and set a fast pace homewards. The mood was dejected and neither felt like talking. They had not gone far when suddenly Aipi froze and pointed into a tree. Kisoo hardly dared to believe it, but yes, there was the slightest flick of a tail. Without hesitation, the two boys slipped their arrows into their bows and sped them on their way.

Thud! A fine, large possum crashed through the branches and lay dead at their feet. Quickly they cut down a stout branch, slung the large furry animal from it and carried it between them. All thought of returning the bow had fled from Kisoo's mind. He wanted the whole world to know of their kill. His home was the nearest, so Aipi had conceded that they should take it there. He began to chant as they went along!

'The possum is dead oo!
Softly it crept oo!
Silently it hid oo!
With my bright eye I saw it!
With my strong bow I shot it!
A fine fat possum oo oo oo!'

The song carried over the mountain, to the man house. Kisoo's brothers had just woken and were busy uncovering the embers and blowing them into a flame. Smoke was seeping through the thatch and mingling with the cloud which lay like a cloak over the cluster of houses. But now, hearing the victory chant, they crowded to get out of the low doorway.

There was a chatter and a chirping from the women's houses too. As usual Mondo, the little blind girl, managed to get in everyone's way, and they were falling over her in their excitement.

Kisoo was delighted when he saw the little bodies, tumbling out from the houses, and crying with admiration. 'Ei! Ei! Fine possum!' and his brothers clicked their fingers from their mouths as one did when one saw a thing of wonder. But then Mata, older than Kisoo and jealous of his success, drew attention to the bow.

'That isn't your bow! That is the bow of the stranger. You are a thief! A thief!'

"No! No! I made one like it. It is mine.' Kisoo was adamant, but so was Mata. The others joined in, voices and tempers rising. The possum lay forgotten on the ground as Mata seized the bow and the boys struggled for possession. The others closed in, shouting excitedly. Suddenly, in one terrible moment, the bow snapped! There was an awful silence as Kisoo gazed in horror.

'Kisoo is a thief.' It was Kepa, his small brother and devoted follower, who spoke. The words were said more in fear than in condemnation. And how could he deny it now? Kisoo turned and ran. His father would beat him; might even slit his ear, thus branding him for life. A thief! He didn't know where he was running to. He had nowhere to go. He only knew that he must run away.

2

OVER THE MOUNTAIN

The blood was pounding in his head as Kisoo ran, blindly, not caring where he was going. His chest hurt as his breath came in short, ragged gasps. Already he could imagine his father calling the village elders. He could hear the thud of their feet as they pursued him. They would surround him, beat him with sticks; and then slit his ear with a sliver of bamboo. He had seen this done to a boy from another clan, and vividly remembered his shame.

Kisoo stumbled on, crying out in fear as his foot caught in a bramble and flung him to the ground. He lay winded, helpless and sobbing.

No, there was no sound. He must have imagined it. But they would come. Struggling to his feet, he took off once more. There was nowhere to go and he would surely have to return sometime, but these thoughts were pushed away as he raced further away from the village.

A thorn bush stretched out angry branches to

scratch him. The bog must have reached out as he sought to leap from tuft to grassy tuft, and he found himself knee deep in the oozing mud. Kisoo was a child of the forest, he had negotiated dense thickets in the moonlight and returned unscathed. But now all nature was angry, or was it the evil spirits who were abroad, seeking to punish him for breaking the conventions of their tribe? He sobbed in fear as he struggled through the mire and then began a long climb upward. Without realising it, he had come to the great escarpment that walled them in from the outside world.

The air was getting thinner now, and a faintness came over him. He was still climbing, higher and yet higher. Cautiously he emerged into a clearing and looked down. He was above the clouds now. How beautiful they were in their snowy whiteness, the sun shining upon them. Somewhere below him was a cluster of houses that had always been his home, his world. They would be pulling out the sweet potatoes that he had helped to prepare the night before. Kisoo clutched his stomach. No good thinking of that.

He looked up the cliff that rose up far above him. How often he and his brothers had gazed up there and one or the other would boast, 'I will go hunting for cassowary there when I am a man.' But they all knew that of course they wouldn't go, for 'Are there not cannibals in the valley beyond?' 'Don't ever go there,' Mother had said. 'They will eat you.'

But in stubbornness the boy continued to climb. 'I won't go back! I won't!' he affirmed. 'It was Mata's fault. He broke the bow.' Sadly he thought about the fine possum they had killed. 'Aipi will have taken it back to his people,' he sighed, 'and they will have a feast.' But it didn't do to think about food. He stumbled on and up.

The sun must have been at its highest point as he reached the summit, but now, the clouds were rolling in and forming a great grey curtain across the landscape. 'A big rain is coming,' Kisoo muttered and ran helter skelter down the other side, looking for cover. The rain would bring cold and he knew he could die of exposure.

He ran until he came to a patch of cultivated ground. There must be houses close by for Kisoo had caught just a whiff of the acrid smell of wood smoke. As the large, icy drops of rain began to lash down, he found a garden shelter and crept under it for cover.

The boy snuggled down, covering himself as best he could with the leaves and branches that lay there.

'Oh, if only I dare run to a house for shelter, or even to ask for an ember to make myself a fire,' he sighed. 'But I know I must not.' He tried to sleep, but hunger was gripping and twisting his stomach.

After what seemed like many hours there was a lull in the rain and Kisoo crept out, desperate to find some food. At last he came upon a clump of sugar cane and cut off some stems with his stone axe.

'Now I am indeed a thief,' he muttered, for to steal from another's garden was breaking the unwritten law of the mountain people. He sucked hungrily at its sugar, crunching up the fibres with his strong teeth before spitting them out.

'I must try to sleep now.' Kisoo knew his stomach would not be satisfied for long. 'Perhaps if I crawl right down under the leaves, the spirits will not know that I am here.'

Sleep was long in coming and, lying in the blackness, his thoughts turned to Mondo, the strange girl who had clouds instead of bright jewels for eyes. What must it be like for her? With darkness there was always fear, and hers was a life of perpetual night. At least he knew that morning would come.

When he awoke next, it was to the sound of singing. He listened intently. It was children's voices, and yes, he could understand it. It was not some strange language as he might have expected, though it was a little different from the way the people of his village spoke. He tried to catch the words.

'That good friend Jesus.' The song droned on tonelessly, but it sounded good to him.

'Where am I?' he thought. Then he remembered,

- the shame of the broken bow, and his flight. In his heart he knew that it was foolish, for surely he would have to go back some time. And now here he was, far over the mountain, in alien territory.

'I am here now, and yet they speak our language. And who is singing? And who is this they are singing about? I must go and see.'

He crawled out, cutting a bunch of leaves and fixing them into his belt. He did not intend to let himself be seen, and crept quietly along until he came upon a small house, built apart from some others.

A man sat in the doorway, while a group of children squatted around him. They looked the same kind of mountain people as he was - and yet there was something different about them. Their skin was brown and shiny and their hair short like fur, not all tufted and tousled as his was.

The man was wearing the most interesting covering he had ever seen. He did not have the usual belt made from vines, or the cloth that hung as an apron in front and the bunch of leaves at the back. The upper part of him was covered with something that was brightly coloured, like some of the feathers of a bird of paradise. And below his belt was something that came down to his knees and seemed to go all round. He wished he could go up and feel it.

The man was telling the children a story. 'It happened like that,' he would say, as they did when telling their own folk tales, and yet this was not any story that Kisoo had ever heard. And there were many things in the story that he did not understand. He talked about an animal, like a large pig, that a man could sit on. Whoever heard of such a thing? But the story was about this man Jesus, the one they had been singing about. Kisoo wanted to know who he was. Did he come from that side of the mountain too?

They sang some more songs, and then the children ran off. The man went back inside his house and Kisoo could hear him blowing up his fire into a blaze. The boy could have found a spot in the sun to warm himself, but a fire meant comfort, and food, and somehow he could not tear himself away.

After a while the man came out through the low doorway and stood up. 'Come, boy!' he called. 'Come for the purpose of eating.'

Kisoo was amazed. He didn't think anyone had seen him there, crouching in the bushes. But he should have known that this man too had the keen eyes of a hunter. Sheepishly, he stood up. He had no mirror. The only image he had ever seen of himself was in a deep puddle after the rain. Somehow he knew that he did not compare favourably with this stranger, or with the children that had been there. His hair was a tousled mop, his skin caked with a mixture of ash and mud and tears. He wanted food desperately, yet fear still held him back. 'Never wander into the territory of another tribe, and never, never accept food from a stranger.'

The man broke off a piece of sweet potato and began to eat. 'It isn't poisoned,' he assured him. 'Come and eat.' Cautiously Kisoo edged over to join him, and then the two of them went into the house.

'I am a stranger here myself,' he volunteered. I have come to live among this clan so that I can teach them the good news, the news about God and his Son Jesus.'

'Is that, "That good friend, Jesus?"' Kisoo asked. Jon, for that was his name, looked surprised.

'I heard you singing the song,' Kisoo explained.

'Yes, I will tell you about him, but first we will eat, and then I want you to tell me how it is that you have come here, for this isn't your territory, is it?'

'I will tell you,' the boy began. He didn't want to drag out the sorry tale, but he was warm now and his stomach was beginning to feel satisfied. After all, it was a story to tell; but he was still uneasy.

'You said that you are a stranger here, and I am a stranger. Do you think it is safe for us to sit like this in the house without any guard? They could creep up on us and take us by surprise. They are cannibals, you know.'

And just then he leaped up in fear.

3

KISOO FINDS A FRIEND

Jon crept cautiously to the door, then laughed as he found a group of wide-eyed youngsters peering in, ready to take flight.

'Oh, so you want to know who the stranger is, do you, and if he has come to eat you?' he said gently.

'I eat them?' Kisoo exclaimed in indignation. He could not help wondering at the way this man had spoken to the children. Others might have taken a stick from the fire to chase them away. And then he laughed. 'Perhaps their mothers tell them the same as our mothers tell us.'

'Ei! Ei!' The children were snapping their fingers from their mouths in wonder. 'Ei! He is an ugly one!'

'Yes, yes, and you are ugly too if you do not wash and have your hair cut. I must teach him, the same as I am teaching you. Off with you now, and if you are good tomorrow, I will blow on the conch shell to call you, and maybe the stranger will tell you his story.'

'What is this you are saying - wash?' Kisoo asked when he had sent the children away. 'And what about their hair? And - what is this that covers you?' and he reached out to touch Jon's shirt.

Again Jon's laugh welled up as from a hidden spring. 'I have so much to teach you. Come, I had better satisfy your curiosity and I have to fetch water and firewood before the rain comes.'

He covered over the fire with ash, picked up an axe and a gourd, and slung a string bag from his shoulder. A plank was pulled across the doorway as they left.

Kisoo followed Jon down a forest trail and the two halted by a mountain stream. They both drank from a spout that had been left there and filled the gourd. Then the boy watched, amazed, as Jon took off his shirt and stepped into the stream. He had taken something yellow from his bag and Kisoo saw him rub it to make a lather.

'Ei! Ei! Magic!' Kisoo cried, but he was beginning to understand the secret of the shiny skin of these people.

'This is white man's medicine,' Jon explained. 'It helps to keep away the sickness. You won't get sores if you wash like this every day,' he told him, pointing to the ulcer on Kisoo's leg. 'Come! Come!' he coaxed and eventually Kisoo stepped into the water and some of the layers of dirt were washed away.

'We have been blaming the evil spirits for our sickness,' Jon explained, after they had left the river and were chopping firewood.

'But we can protect ourselves from disease by keeping clean. We must cut our hair and not let the lice live there. I will show you. And we must dig toilet holes - away from our houses. All these things I will teach you. You didn't know you would learn so many new things when you climbed the mountain, did you?'

Again the joyous laugh bubbled up as though he knew some wonderful secret.

'And this?' Kisoo again fingered the shirt that had also been washed and was now drying in the sun.

'This, like the soap, is something that the white man has brought. But they have given us something more precious than any of these things.'

'White man? What is white man?' How could there be so many things to ask, Kisoo wondered.

'I will try to answer all your questions,' Jon said, gathering up the firewood. 'But look! The clouds are already closing in and the rain will be coming. Let us go back to the house and then we can both tell our stories.'

When they returned there was an offering of sweet potato and some corn left for the teacher. Gratefully they brought it in and were soon sitting by the fire, their food cooking in the ash.

'Now,' encouraged the man. 'First you tell me what made you come into this territory, and then I will tell you my story.'

And so Kisoo began. 'Aipi and I are brothers,' he began. He didn't mention stealing the bow of the stranger. 'It was I who spied the possum,' he went on, making sure that he got all the glory, but when he got to the part where Mata called him a thief Kisoo knew that he needed to give some explanation.

'It was all my brother's fault,' he blazed. 'It was he who gave me shame. I had to run away or they might have called the elders to beat me and slit my ear. And so I climbed right up the mountain and came here. It happened like that,' he concluded.

Jon sat quietly before he spoke.

'You should not have taken the bow. You did even more wrong to run away and come into strange territory when you had been forbidden. And yet I believe that even in this God was guiding you. You have come here for a purpose.'

Kisoo's eyes opened wide. He knew that there was a God who had made the earth, but how could this God know about one young boy?

The teacher was continuing. 'You say that your brother gave you shame, but you bring it upon yourself when you do things which are wrong. God's book says, *Do not steal*, and he is pleased with us when we try to do as he asks.'

'God's book! What is God's book?' Kisoo asked. He watched, wide eyed, amazed, as Jon reached up into the rafters above his head and pulled out a small bundle. Carefully he unwrapped it. 'This is part of God's book.'

Kisoo came close and peered at it. It was not like anything he had seen before. He wanted to ask so many questions, but Jon silenced him. It was his turn to tell his story now, and he must not be interrupted.

'All around our villages are high mountains. The people of this valley did not know about your clans. I did not know about these people. And none of us knew about the people beyond the mountains and they did not know about us.

'Then one day some white men climbed over the mountains. They told us, "Make a piece of ground flat and smooth, and we will come again and bring you many good things." And so they came again in a big bird they call an aeroplane. They brought us this soap to wash, and razor blades to cut our hair. They brought us clothes like I am wearing and plants that we could grow for better food.

'But best of all, they brought us God's book so that we can know God and not live in fear of the evil spirits all the time.

'A white man came to my village. He called the elders and asked for someone to help him write God's book in our language. I and some others promised to help him. As we worked together, I found that God was speaking to me through this book. I learned that God has a Son, Jesus.'

'That good friend, Jesus?' Kisoo asked. He could not help interrupting now.

Jon nodded. 'He came from heaven to live on this earth. He came to save us. We have all broken God's laws - the laws written in God's book. Do not steal, do not lie, do not murder, and many others. Because of this we are God's enemies. But so that we can become his friends, his children, his own Son, Jesus, took our punishment.

'You said that your punishment would have been a beating and maybe slitting your ear.' Kisoo began to tremble at the thought of it. 'Well, God's punishment for breaking his laws is death. We must go to the place of darkness and burning. But because he loves us and wants to save us, he sent his Son, Jesus, to take our place. Jesus was killed so that God can forgive you, if you ask him.'

'My father wouldn't forgive me,' declared Kisoo. But then he added, 'Of course - he might forget, - but not for a long time. And I can't stay here for a long time. These people might decide to have a feast - and eat me.'

'Listen, Kisoo.' Jon had replaced the book and was pulling the sweet potato from the fire. 'I have asked God to forgive me and that is why I am not afraid to come and live among these people. Was I afraid to tell you my name, in case it gave you power over me? I know that Jesus is with me and he is stronger than every evil power.

'Every day I have looked at these mountains that you crossed. I have asked God for a way to go to the people living on the other side, so that I can tell them about him.

'Kisoo, you have got to go back to your own place, but I want to come with you. I will help you to make another bow, a very good one to give to the stranger, and we will ask your father to forgive you. I will tell your people that the men from the government are coming soon to write their names in a book. Then they will have to keep the new laws. And the white man's law says, No more cutting off fingers and noses.'

'Or slitting ears?' Kisoo whispered, hardly daring to believe.

'No, no slitting ears,' he confirmed. 'But most of all I want to tell them about God's book and that God wants them to walk in His road. 'What do you think, Kisoo? Will you come with me and lead me to your people?'

Kisoo sat quietly for a long time. He took a stick and stirred the fire into a blaze. He knew he could not go on running away, always hiding, always living in fear. And yet, had he the courage to go back to his people? If he showed this stranger the way to their village, they might be even more angry with him. What should he do?

4

BACK HOME WITH A STRANGER

Kisoo made a swift gesture with his nose, to indicate to Jon that they were at last in sight of his home. They paused to look up together at the great trees, that stood as sentinel around his village. These mountain people always built high up, in case an enemy should creep up on them unawares. They both knew that warriors would be standing at the ready, their bodies pressed into the hollows that had been carved into the great trunks. Arrows would be fitted to their bows, for was he not bringing a stranger into their midst?

Jon stood quietly, waiting for Kisoo to begin the ascent. One could only go in single file on these mountain paths. As the boy still did not move, he stepped forward and peered over his shoulder to see what was wrong. A tiny lizard was resting on a twig before them, enjoying the watery sun that had struggled through the clouds. Sensing movement, it disappeared in a flash, and the spell that had transfixed Kisoo was broken. He began to dance about in anguish.

'Ei! Ei!' he cried. 'It is an evil sign. I should never have let you to come with me.' But the man's hand was on his shoulder.

'Our good friend Jesus, has come to free us from fear of all these things. That little lizard is beautiful. It is no longer a thing of fear.'

Kisoo paused to gaze at him. 'You are not afraid?'

'No,' Jon confirmed, 'I am not afraid. Come, call out and tell them that we are coming.'

They had set out on their journey in the first light of the morning. The clouds had been lying as a blanket over the valleys and it seemed as if the whole world was swathed in mystery. How glad they had been to feel the sun's warmth on their bodies, as the clouds melted away.

'Ei! It is so steep. I wonder that I ever found my way up here safely,' Kisoo remarked as they had searched for the safest way down.

'Yes,' agreed Jon. 'But I believe that God was guiding you.'

He had prayed far into the night for this boy, who had come so suddenly among them. It was indeed answered prayer that Kisoo should be leading him to his tribe.

Kisoo's eyes were downcast now, for he was

fearing the wrath of his father for bringing a stranger into their midst. But now, at last, in the pale light of the evening sun, he knew that he could not run away any more. He had promised to bring the teacher to his village, and there was no turning back. He raised his hands above his head. 'Oy, oo oo!' he yodelled. Immediately the children were running down the track.

'Kisoo is coming! Kisoo is coming! From where are you coming oo?' they sang out in response.

'I and the teacher are coming from a far place oo,' was his reply.

Kisoo knew that the watchers would still be standing silently, their bows at the ready, but the children were tumbling down the hillside toward them. The tension was broken as they continued their sing song of conversation.

By the time they had reached the grassy area between the houses, the women were busy sweeping away the droppings from the pigs. They knew that everyone would soon be sitting down and that there would be much talk.

Andupi, Kisoo's father, stood dark and glowering outside the man house. Jon remained on the edge of the green, but Kisoo strode boldly forward.

'Father, truly I did a bad thing to take the bow of the stranger and to run away. But see, I have made a new, good bow to give back to him.'

His father took the bow but spat, as if to say, What was the good of the bow now? The stranger was long gone, and it was too late to wipe out the shame Kisoo had brought them. But Kisoo hurried on before his father should have a chance to speak.

'Father,' he began again, 'this man helped me to make the bow. He has come with me because he has a wonderful thing called a book. It tells us the words of the great Spirit who made the sky and the mountains. This man does not fear the evil spirits.'

At this Andupi held up a hand to silence his son. His voice came out as a roar.

'What lying talk is this you are speaking? What man is there who dares to say that he does not fear the spirits?' Again he spat, emphatically.

But Jon had stepped forward now. 'No,' he said, 'It is not lying talk. It is true talk. Let me tell you.'

Andupi indicated to the whole clan which had gathered, and they squatted down on the grass in a circle. Jon sat down beside him.

Kisoo could not help but compare the two men. His father was renowned as a great warrior. Was he not known as Andupi, killer of eight? Pepona, his youngest wife, had been bringing her pigs home from the bush when one had run off. Leaving the others with a lad, she had run off in pursuit. 'It happened like that,' they said.

The pig had strayed into the garden of another

clan, and a woman had accused Pepona of stealing her pig. The two women struggled, clawing and scratching each other. Andupi had come home that evening to hear the wailing of the women, for Pepona had returned home, faint and bleeding, and, worst of all, without the piglet.

The next thing they knew, her husband was towering over his wife. He had put on his wig, and painted his face and body so that he was a fearsome sight. A stone axe was in his belt, and a bow on his shoulder.

'Die, then, woman!' he had shouted. 'You stay there and die! But they will pay for this.' He had stalked away in anger, beating his kundu drum.

This was their way. A life for a life. There must be a payback killing. The woman had fled to the men screaming for protection when she heard of Andupi's approach. But so great had been his wrath, a whole family had been wiped out that night. Yes, Andupi, killer of eight, he was called.

Yes, indeed he was strong, a mighty one, but the face that peered out from the tangle of hair, was full of fear and darkness. Maybe this younger man had not asserted his manhood by killing, but surely he had proved himself strong by coming among unknown people.

They were quiet now as he began to speak. 'When I was born, my mother called me Ugly One.'

'Uh! Uh!' Amusement rippled among the people.

'Ugly one! She thought that with such a name the spirits would not come and trouble me. But then I heard God's words that are written in his book. I know now that God's Son, Jesus, is greater than any bad spirit.

'My name is not Ugly One any more. My name is Jon - the one sent by God. And God has sent me to you because he does not want you to live in fear either.'

'Book? What is this book?' It was Yayowana, Kisoo's sister, who asked, and no one silenced her. They all wanted to know. Excitedly, Kisoo interrupted, trying to explain.

'Truly, Father, it is something very wonderful. It is like leaves, only clay coloured, and it has many markings on it, like the marks that birds make with their feet. The teacher looks at the marks and they tell him stories, like our old men tell.'

'No one tells stories like our old men,' one cried, and they all joined in agreement.

'No! No! It is true,' Kisoo affirmed. 'Only let Jon bring the book and you will see. It is truly our talk and our ways. You will see.'

Jon sat quietly, listening and waiting as the conversation flowed, to and fro. These mountain people loved talking, for they spent long hours sitting around their fires, and this was how they passed their time. Now here, in the last light of day, everyone had to be given a chance to speak, even the young boys.

As they were talking, Jon was quietly praying that they would accept this wonderful opportunity that was coming to them. Even as he prayed, again this joy which had sustained him through loneliness and opposition began to well up within his heart. He was remembering the many hours that he had spent with the missionary, seeking to find just the right word, the right expression, so that the people would really be able to understand.

'Why is it?' Karl had reasoned. 'When I write their stories and then read them to the people, they do not listen to this word?' And he had prayed and rewritten. 'Don't you see,' he had exclaimed at last, 'we have to make it sound like their stories, otherwise they will never accept it.'

And what was it that Kisoo had said? 'It tells stories like our old men tell.' Truly God had helped them.

But now Andupi was on his feet and had clapped his hands. There was silence up there on that mountain top. The mothers were putting babies to their breasts in case they should disturb this solemn moment.

Jon stepped forward in response to his gesture of

command. In spite of the assurance that God had led him, his legs were shaking. He knew that unless every one of them had agreed he would never be allowed to come again. What would their response be? Would they come to know Jesus as their friend, or continue living as they had always done?

5

THE BOOK

'The teacher is coming oo - oo - oo!' The call rang out from far away over the mountains. Kisoo threw down the bundle of wood he had been carrying and raced down to the river to wash himself. He wanted to be the first to welcome Jon, but must show him that he was following the ways he had been taught. He did not want to be ashamed.

The evangelist had no means of telling them when he was coming. The day he arrived was the day for 'church', for hearing the good talk.

'From where are you coming oo?' Kisoo welcomed Jon as he made his final ascent up the mountain.

'I come from far places, where I have been teaching God's word,' he responded. Like the Pied Piper he had gathered the children behind him. Now he shooed them off to wash too, making sure that Mondo was not left behind this time.

He had noticed the girl the first time he had

visited the village. As he had waited for Andupi's reaction to his request, he had been aware of a rasping breath, the sound the highlanders make to denote a great effort. He had glanced down to see a girl, tears pouring from her sightless eyes, struggling to feel her way back to safety. He could do nothing about it then, but he made sure that she was not forgotten this time.

Passing the area where the cluster of houses were, they continued climbing until they reached another clearing.

'It is finished?' he questioned, as he gazed at the church that they had built. Andupi and the other men were gathering around him, beaming.

'Nearly,' they assured him.

'Truly, you have done well,' Jon commended them, his face alight.

'This new axe you brought us, a gift from the white man, truly it is a thing of wonder. We could not have done the work so quickly without it.'

'Never have we built a house like this before. We had to find very tall casuarina trees.'

'True! True! We build our houses low to keep warm. But here we will have no fire, for we will only meet in the day. And many people will come. Some of the other clans came to help us. They are all coming to hear the good talk.'

Jon's heart was glowing as he sat to rest while the

people hurried off to wash and clothe themselves. Grass skirts for the women, a fresh bunch of leaves for the men. Some of the old men put on their great wigs, but the younger men were proud of their new hair style. Jon had introduced them to the wonder of the razor blade and now with their hair shiny from the application of water and a bamboo comb they were resplendent.

'Ask your father to give the second call, so that we can begin church,' Jon told Kisoo. 'The sun is already high in the sky and the rain will be here before I am on my way, and I have far to go.' But Andupi laughed when Kisoo passed on the message.

'We must wait until all the people have gathered. Do not worry. We have prepared a house for you. And see, we have lit a fire so that we can heat the stones, and cook some food in an earth oven. This is a special day.'

At last he set the conch shell to his lips and blew the long wail that echoed over the mountains. Then the people stood up and quietly began to enter the building, awe on their faces. Some of the women came with gifts from their gardens and laid it at the front. It was all they had to bring, and Jon had been teaching them to bring an offering to God.

Crouching on the stones that had been placed as seats, Jon led them in their toneless singing. 'That good friend Jesus' - that was the song that Kisoo liked the best. Then Jon prayed. He did not use the name that they had known for God, but he called him, 'Father.' This is a thing of wonder, thought Kisoo. Truly there were many things he wanted to know.

Jon opened the book, this wonderful thing that was God's gift to them. But before he began to read he spoke to them.

'I am glad that you have all gathered here today to hear God's word. I am very happy to see the way you have all worked so hard to build a house of worship. You are all here because as clans you have decided to listen to the good talk. You have agreed for me to come and to teach you. But it is not enough for your tribe to hear the good talk. You must each one receive God's word into you own heart. Each one of you must eat it yourself, and God will give you a new heart. This is the only way that you can be in God's kingdom.

'Listen! I am going to tell you a story from God's book. It is a story about a garden.'

He had their attention now. The children playing on the floor were poked into silence, the babies put to their breasts. Gardens were the most important part of their lives, next to pigs. They wanted to hear this story.

'A man went out to plant seed in his garden,' he began, but then he went on to explain that it was a very big garden so he had to take the seed and scatter it.

'We would never do such a foolish thing,' thought Kisoo. 'We plant each seed or each tuber carefully. No wonder many of his seeds did not grow. But ours, of course they grow.'

Jon went on to tell the sad story of how some of the seeds he planted did not grow well. 'God wants each one of you to eat his word. He wants it to grow in each of your lives so that you will be changed and grow to be like his Son Jesus.'

Later in the day it was time to open the earth oven. There was no pig today. It had to be a very special celebration for that, but there were pandanus nuts and vegetables. It was harvest time, and there was a spirit of joy as they all sat round on the grass.

'Not many moons now and the elders will be taking us into the forest for our initiation ceremonies,' Aipi confided, as the boys sat together.

'Ei!' exclaimed Bee. 'I wonder what feats we will have to perform?' There was a shiver of fear in his voice.

'Never mind that. It will be over soon enough and then we'll come back and decorate ourselves and do our tribal dances, and all the girls will be after us.'

God's word was quite forgotten.

But towards evening Kisoo's mother sent him to the garden with his sister to fetch food for the next day.

'Ei! It was very hard work to cut down the trees

and clear the ground for the garden,' Kisoo boasted, for had he not helped? 'Truly it is man's work.'

'Yes, and it is very hard work to dig these round mounds for our gardens and plant the food,' countered his sister. 'You work once and boast about it for the rest of your lives, but we have to work every day.'

She expected a response, for there was fun in an argument, but Kisoo was silent. 'What is it?' she asked.

'I was thinking about what the teacher told us about the man planting his garden.'

'Yes, truly, was not that foolishness, to throw seed on the ground for the birds to eat? We don't make gardens like that. Our seeds grow.'

'Yes, I know. That is what I was thinking, but here - look! See! Someone has stepped on this sweet potato vine, and it has withered. It won't grow now. And look at this bean. A worm has eaten it. It is dead.'

He was silent, pondering as they dug up some of the tubers, but when he came to gather the corn that Jon had taught them to grow, he began to laugh. A joyous chuckle welled up from within him.

'What is it?' Yayowana asked.

'Look at this! Seven fine corn on one plant! All that from one seed.'

'I want to have much corn in my life,' he added,

but he did not say this aloud. He was thoughtful, thinking about the plants that had died. That night he lay by the fire, but he was not sleeping.

'Suppose God's word does not grow in me? Then I will not have that good friend Jesus to protect me, and those bad spirits that we have always feared will have power over me. How can I be sure that God's word will grow in my life?'

As soon as the first grey light of dawn began to creep through the grass walls of the man house Kisoo slipped out and went to where Jon was already awake and stirring up his fire.

'May I come in?' Kisoo called softly.

'Come!' was the response.

'I am troubled about the story you told us,' Kisoo confided. 'How can I be sure that God's word will grow in my heart?'

Jon sat for a while, wondering how best to answer him. Then he pulled a sweet potato from the ash, broke off a piece and handed it to Kisoo.

'Kisoo,' he said, 'Yesterday we had a feast, but today we are hungry again. Suppose we only ate when we had a feast?'

The lad was dismayed. He knew that they needed to eat many pounds of the tuber to get enough nourishment to live. 'We would die,' he affirmed.

Jon wiped his hands, then reached out to his net bag and unwrapped his Bible. 'When I come here I read to you the stories from God's book. I am happy that you listen well. Not everyone listens as you do. But God's word is like food for our spirit. If we are going to be strong Christians, to let God's life in us grow strongly, then we must read this book every day.'

'Then you will stay here with us and teach us every day?' Kisoo was excited. 'We will make you gardens. I will tell my father.'

Jon laughed. 'Kisoo, there are many other people besides your clan who have to be taught. I cannot stay here. And, not many moons hence, you will be going away to your other gardens and I will not be able to visit you there.

'But listen! You can learn to read! You can have your own book. Then you can read it every day, even when you travel to your other gardens and I am not able to visit you; and you will grow to be a strong Christian and will be able to teach the others in your family.'

Kisoo came and peered over Jon's shoulder at the strange markings in the book. Was it possible that it could ever tell him stories as it did to Jon? 'How could I learn to read?' he asked, his big brown eyes opened wide.

'I will teach you if you are willing to learn. Listen, Kisoo, when I leave here I am going home to my own place, for it is time for me to go and help my wife make new gardens. I must cut more firewood for her, so that she has enough while I am away. I shall stay there for one moon. If you will come with me, I will teach you every day.'

Kisoo was excited! To be able to read this wonderful book, God's book! Was it possible that he could learn?

But there was fear in his heart too, for it would mean going into alien territory again, among strange people. He had done it once, but only because he had been angry and afraid. But he wouldn't be going in shame this time. He would be going because he wanted to serve 'that good friend Jesus', and to read his word.

Jon sat quietly, praying. If only Kisoo would agree to come with him. He knew that his life could be changed, as his own had been when he had studied the Bible day by day. But he knew it wasn't an easy decision for the boy to make.

'What do you say?' he asked at last. 'Shall we go and ask you father?'

6

MONDO

'Aii!- Aii! - Aii!' The thin, high-pitched wailing pierced through the damp clouds that were still enfolding the little village on the side of the mountain. It reached the women who were waiting for the sun to break through before they would take their pigs to pasture.

'Oh, that blind one! She is always crying! I suppose the children have been teasing her again,' said Kainowana as she spat into the fire.

'The children are cruel. They wave branches in front of her face to make her think that the evil spirits are after her.' It was Tanona who spoke.

Her mother rounded on her. 'Cruel, are they? And who was it who put a beetle on her leg and told her that it was a poisonous spider?'

The girl hid her face, giggling nervously.

'No light in her eyes! What good is she? Why didn't they leave her to die?' The words came from Ayu, the old one. She too was put in her place.

'You look out, old one. They'll be leaving you to die before long. She can carry a bag of sweet potato and dig her garden with the best of us. You won't be able to do that much longer.'

Now it was the old one's turn to wail. She knew that it was true and she was afraid. Would they leave her behind when they moved across the mountains?

Her daughter reached into the ash for a sweet potato. She handed a piece to her mother. There is nothing like food in the mouth to administer comfort. The other piece she gave to Kepa. 'Here, son, go and give this to Mondo and find out why she is crying. Bring her back to the fire to warm herself.'

She watched the little boy run off. She knew that he could probably do more than she could, for she would have lost patience and shouted or beaten the girl, and it would have had no effect. Eh! She is a stubborn one, that one. But maybe a little child could coax her.

Of course, had not she herself been coaxed when Mondo had first been brought to her? Yes, it was true, for she should have been left to die. She must have been abandoned by her own people, and yet she had somehow won her brother's heart when he had found her. He had been hunting one night and had come upon her sitting, trailing her fingers in the water beside a stream. Her sightless eyes did not know night from day, and, not seeing the arrow fitted to his bow, she had held out her little arms expectantly. The next thing he knew, he had gathered her up and she was seated upon his shoulders.

'Fool!' she muttered, and spat again at the memory. 'A pig, yes, but to bring a blind child to me!' But she too had been made foolish, for the little girl had reached out to her in response to her voice and was soon snuggled to her breast. 'Of course, I was mourning for my little one that had died, and I had milk to spare - but a blind one!'

'Shall we come in?' a little voice called, after a while, but as Kepa moved the covering from the doorway to bring the blind girl in, the women saw that the sun was breaking through and it was time to lead their pigs out and set off for their gardens.

'Come, Mondo, I will lead you.' The tears were not far away, and the little boy seemed to understand her need of comfort. Of course, if he had been old enough to sleep in the man house he would never have thought of helping a girl like this; but though he was maybe six years old, he was still allowed to drink from his mother's breast, still allowed to show the tenderness of a child.

'It's alright, Kepa,' she answered. 'You walk in front and I will follow. I know the paths around here. I can feel the way with my stick.'

'That is why I am so frightened of having to travel to our new gardens. I won't know any of the paths.'

They were still talking about it as they sat that evening munching the sugar cane that one of the men had harvested from his garden.

'I have learned the paths around here,' Mondo explained. 'I have learned to listen and to smell. I know where the steep places are where I might fall over the mountain. I know where the plants with the sharp thorns are that might pierce my feet.'

'I will lead you, Mondo. I will give you my hand.'

A smile curled across her lips but her empty eyes were turned upwards. She was silent. Then, 'There are swift flowing rivers to cross. You will need someone to help you, Kepa. They will forget all about me.'

Kepa crunched off a piece of the sugar cane and taking it from his own mouth stuffed it into hers. He didn't want the girl to start crying again.

'And suppose we have to cross the vine bridge that swings and sways over the great river,' she began again as soon as she could speak. 'If I slipped from that I would be swept away and never be seen again.'

'You wouldn't slip,' Kepa admonished. 'Your feet are strong and sure, like mine. And in any case, Kisoo says that we are not going the way of the vine bridge.'

'Oh, Kepa! You don't understand.' She reached out to pat his hand, but Kepa was gone, wearying of his effort to cheer her.

'Why is Mondo so frightened of leaving here?' Kepa had asked his older brother as they had run to the river together for water. 'I promised to hold her hand.'

'You look out, or you will never grow up to be a mighty warrior like Father,' Kisoo warned. 'Sons of Andupi, the mighty one, do not hold girls' hands.' As he said it, a thought came to him. He sat down suddenly on the bank of the river, a gourd between his knees. 'Andupi, killer of eight,' he mused. 'Maybe that has a lot to do with her fear.'

'Why? Father wouldn't kill her. She is our family!'

'No! No! Father wouldn't kill her. But because he killed that clan we always have to be on guard in case they come to pay back the killings. A blind girl - or a small boy - that would be easy pray for them.'

'But, - he killed them all, didn't he?' Kepa's voice faltered as he faced the awful possibility.

'He thought he did, yes, but we can never be sure.' He turned threateningly to the little boy. 'So, you be careful!' he warned. 'No running off on your own! And never, never accept help from a stranger.'

Even as he repeated these rules that had been laid down for him since he was as small as Kepa, Kisoo realised afresh that he had not only broken the bow, but had broken every rule when he had run away and been taken in by Jon. But how glad he was. Not only had the teacher come among them to teach them God's ways, but now he too had his own book and was learning to read.

'Look, Kisoo! Look!' Kepa exclaimed, some days later as, having left their familiar territory, they had set out on their journey to reclaim their other gardens. 'The girls are trying to wade through the river. Oh! Oh! It is not deep, but it is very swift and strong.'

Hearing screams, the travellers all turned back. They ran to the river bank and watched the girls struggling to keep their balance in the fiercely flowing stream.

'Fools!' exclaimed one. 'Why didn't they cross over the log as we did? There was no need to venture through the water.'

'There was a gasp as one of the girls almost lost her footing. 'It's the blind one, of course,' another answered. 'Her fear of the log was too great.'

Andupi spat. 'Why, every day didn't she walk across the log that makes a path for us through the bog? What difference is there between that and walking over this log across the river?'

Kainowana's voice was shrill with anger as she took up the defence of the one she had fostered.

'The difference is that if she fell off that log she

would only be up to her knees in mud. If she fell from this one she would either be killed by falling on to the rocks or she would be carried away by the current and drowned.'

She stretched out her hand to another to anchor herself and to pull the frightened girls, safely to the bank.

Andupi was leading the way up the steep hillside, but as the boys followed they could still hear the voices of the women, shrilling in anger against poor Mondo. 'If my daughter had been drowned because of you...' he heard one say. Poor Mondo. She was holding on to the stick that Kainowana had fastened to her own net bag for her, struggling to keep up. She tried not to cry out in pain when she bruised her foot on a sharp rock or tore her flesh on a thorn bush. 'If only they couldn't see me as I can't see them,' she thought.

The men had reached a crest on the mountainside and were sitting waiting for the women to join them when they heard a man's voice call out below them. Their eyes searched the bushes but they saw no movement. There was no further sound, but they were in no doubt that they were being watched.

'Oh, Kisoo! I was very afraid,' Kepa had confided when they had at last arrived. But now their houses were unboarded, their fires lit. With warmth and the prospect of food, they felt secure. Once inside the man house, Kisoo took out his book from a net bag. He could not attempt to read it, for the light was fading, but as he tucked it securely into the rafters, it reminded him of his responsibility. He had God's word, and he must be the teacher now.

He remembered the words he had repeated to his brother, 'Jon told us that fear is darkness. The Lord Jesus is the light of the world. He wants to chase away all the darkness from our lives. He told us like that. Don't you remember?' He needed to remember it himself.

He sat for a while, gazing into the flames. The night had come swiftly, throwing its own cloak of darkness over the little community that had come to live on the side of the mountain. They were not afraid because they had fire in their house and the men around them. But wouldn't it be wonderful if there should be no more darkness, no more fear?

As he lay down beside his brothers, the boy relived the adventures of the day. He remembered the terror of the blind girl, unable to brave the log bridge, only to face a far worse enemy in the raging river. He thought of the question Kepa had asked him.

'Kisoo!' he had asked, 'Mondo is in the darkness all the time. Doesn't the Lord Jesus want to chase the darkness out of her life too?'

And Kisoo still didn't know how to answer him.

7

KISOO IS HELPED

Slowly, syllable by syllable, Kisoo sounded out the words. 'Very - early - the - next - morning - Jesus - got - up.' Then he went back and tried to read the passage with meaning. Who is it talking about? What does God want to teach me? he asked himself, as Jon had taught him.

'Very early - but I can't get up any earlier, for it is too cold while the clouds are still covering the mountain,' he complained.

As a clan they had boarded up their houses in the village near the escarpment and come to live high up on the mountains beyond the river. Kisoo had crept out of the man house as soon as the sunlight had begun to filter through the blanket of cloud. He was sitting where he could feel its warmth on his body. Even so he envied those still inside, for he could hear them reviving the fire. They would be eating their sweet potato soon. He had better hurry.

'No Bible, no breakfast.' That was the rule Jon

had made for himself. 'You try to keep it too, Kisoo. Remember that God's word is food for our spirits... If we don't eat it every day we will have no strength to walk in God's road.'

A low chanting was coming from the man house. The boys were sitting around the fire making up songs, as they did when they had their tribal dances; one making up a line, and the others joining in the response. Kisoo tried to concentrate on his reading, but then he heard his own name.

'Kisoo has yellow hair - oo - oo.'

'Truly, he has yellow hair - oo,' they all joined in.

He closed the book, thrusting it into his net bag. Blinded by tears, he stumbled out of earshot.

'It wasn't an easy thing to decide to go with Jon as I did,' he complained to himself. He remembered the feelings of fear as he had set out with Jon to go to his home village. The way unknown, the valley had seemed so deep, the river so broad, the vine bridge that was not only a thing of terror to a blind girl.

He remembered the sense of wonder as he had watched the men clearing ground. They had not just burned and cut down the trees as his people did to make a garden, but actually dug out the tree roots. 'It is for the great bird they call an aeroplane to land,' Jon explained.

It had not been easy to stay in Jon's village. The

people had whispered about this stranger and laughed about the way he talked, but they were not unfriendly. The men had asked him to tell them stories as they sat around their fire, and had taken him on a hunt for the wild pigs that were ravaging their gardens.

There had been other boys who came to the church for the reading lessons.

'Ka ke ki ko ku,' they had chanted, 'ma me mi mo mu.'

He soon learned to recognise the sounds and to join in the chorus, but when it came to joining the sounds together and understanding their meaning, Kisoo was in a mist, and Jon's book was just a jumble of sounds to him.

'You cannot return on your own,' Jon advised him, when the boy expressed his discouragement. 'It wouldn't be safe. And I cannot travel with you until after the new moon.' He turned away. He couldn't let the boy give up now. 'Come,' he said, 'Let us go into the church and pray. The Lord Jesus will help you; I know he will.'

How the light came in Kisoo didn't know. It didn't happen that day, or the next, but suddenly he found that the sounds were joining together to make words.

'Gosanya buku pii kningi lenge,' he sang joyfully. God's book speaks the true talk, our language.

'I was so proud when I came back with Jon and he called me to come and read to the people in church. Truly I knew that the good friend Jesus has helped me.'

'Now you won't have to wait for my visit to hear God's word,' Jon had told the people. 'You must come to the church every evening before the sun goes down, and Kisoo can read you a story from God's book.'

'I wish they would not call me *yellow hair*,' sighed Kisoo. They thought that he was trying to be like a European and their mockery hurt. Kisoo thought about what had happened since arriving here where there wasn't a church. 'Now that it is too far for Jon to come, they have forgotten all about becoming Christians and reading God's word,' he grumbled.

Kisoo was too angry and ashamed to go back to the man house, though perhaps if he had seen the disappointment on the face of the girl he might have received a certain consolation; for whenever Kisoo was reading from the Bible, Mondo made sure that she was within ear-shot. Hers was not the ability to see this wonderful thing called book, but she could hear it, and in hearing she found courage and strength to go on.

The boy had begged some food from his mother and now he was wandering down towards the river.

His brother Kepa, sensing that he needed comfort, padded quietly behind.

Kisoo leapt out onto some rocks that stood firm amid the swirling white water, then held out his hand for Kepa to follow him. Squatting on this island fortress, Kisoo tried to explain his anger.

'They all want the good things the Europeans bring us, axes and razor blades and shirts. Why, only the other day we were talking about making the long journey to the government station. They say you can help them to make their roads, and in return they will give you some of their good things.

'Yet this wonderful thing the white man has brought us, God's book - they are mocking at me because I try to read it. They are not walking in God's road as they promised.'

Kepa did not need to say anything, except to give an occasional grunt. Kisoo understood that he had his sympathy.

Just then they heard someone calling from far away, but with the roar of the angry water they could not make out the words. They sprang to the bank, then swiftly climbed up to an outcrop of rock. They were straining their ears to hear for, to these people of the forest, every sound was of significance.

'Kisoo - oo - oo!' That was plain enough. It was his mother's voice.

'Oo - oo - oo!' he made the response. 'I hear you.'

'The pig is lost. Your father wants you to help him to look for it.'

'I go - oo!' he yodelled back.

'Ei! That is a bad thing,' he confided in his brother. 'The pig is due to have piglets. Kepa, run quickly to the man house to fetch my bow and arrows and my axe. I'll be making towards the ridge,' and he pointed the direction with his nose.

'I go,' the little fellow called, already on his way. He was proud to be helping his brother. 'I'll bring my bow too.' He knew that it was not a good thing to go unprotected, for the wild pigs that roamed the forest could be very fierce.

Together again, they wandered on through the trees. From time to time they would climb to a high spot and call to the other searchers, but there was no sign of the wanderer.

'You'd best go home Kepa,' Kisoo advised after a while, for he could see his brother was flagging and knew that the rain would soon overtake them. 'Mother will be needing you to fetch some firewood,' he added, for he didn't want to hurt his feelings.

And so he went on alone. The forest was dense and dark, the sun long hidden behind the heavy rain clouds. It was not long before the icy rain began to lash down and he took shelter beneath some bushes. Kisoo was shivering with cold and a heaviness was still gripping his heart. He could not shake off the hurt he had felt when listening to his brothers' mocking laughter. After a while the clouds lifted a little and he struggled on wearily, surprised to find himself trembling. A terrible cold seemed to be creeping around him and yet he was breaking out in perspiration. This was more than a natural fear.

'What is it?' he thought to himself. 'The spirits are angry. There must be some graves here, or maybe there is a spirit house nearby and I did not know.' He tried to run, but his legs were like lead. 'I must! I must get out of here!' he told himself. Blinded by fear, he did not see the vine that lay across the path, waiting to trip him.

He lay there for a long time, unable to move. It was impossible to think, let alone cry out. Then, unbidden, as a whisper on the wind, the words were there in his mind, 'I will never leave you.'

It was Jon who had taught him to say this promise of Jesus. 'Say it, Kisoo,' he had told him. 'Say it when you are lonely. Say it when you are afraid.'

'I will never leave you.' Kisoo spoke the words out, softly at first, then louder. He sat up. It was as if the snare that had held him had been broken. He started to rub himself, to bring warmth back into his limbs.

'Oh Jesus,' he whispered, 'Good friend Jesus, this is your promise, never to leave me. Help me? Please help me?'

At last, the fear gone, Kisoo was able to stand up and make a way through the undergrowth. How he knew which direction to go he didn't understand. Then, pushing through another dense thicket, he saw it - a puddle of yellow mud and the wallowing pig, her snout and heaving flank exposed to the air.

Swiftly Kisoo climbed to a high mound and called out, 'The pig is found - oo - oo - oo!' The message was passed from one to the other until little Kepa heard it back in the village. 'I'm sure it was Kisoo who found it,' he said.

Now Kisoo had the problem of coaxing the wanderer back home. Cutting a strong creeper from a tree, he squatted beside the contented animal, pondering the problem.

The rain was still on the hills all around them but just then a watery sun broke through and Kisoo looked up to see a rainbow arching the valley.

'God's bow,' he mused, his heart filled with joy. 'Lord Jesus, you have put your bow in the sky to remind me of your promise. Your's is not as a man's bow that can break. Now I know that you will never leave me. Truly you helped me to find the pig and I know that you will help me to get her home.'

He reached into the mud for the pig's front leg and tied the vine to it. Just then the great animal eased herself out of her bath and began to trot along happily beside her captor.

'Oh, Lord Jesus,' again he prayed. He wasn't saying his prayers as Jon had taught him, but rather talking to a friend alongside. 'You have helped me today. You have saved me from the bad spirits that made me so afraid. You have helped me to find the pig and to bring her home.'

He walked on quietly for a while, realising slowly that he must let his wonderful friend bring light into every situation. At last he put it into words. 'Lord Jesus,' he prayed, 'Will you help me to read your book, so that the others in my tribe will listen to your word too?' He knew that it was a big thing to ask. Was 'that good friend Jesus' able to do even this?'

8

THE FIRE

'Kisoo?'

The boy recognised his brother's voice calling him. It was a crisp, golden morning and the sunlight was already peeping in through the thatch. On such a day it was no hardship to leave the ash and smoke of the man house.

'Yo!' Kisoo laughed, seeing anticipation sparkling in his little brother's eyes. 'Yes, it is a good morning. We will go today. You go and prepare yourself. Give me a few minutes to read God's book and then we will go.'

'I will bring food. We can eat on the way,' Kepa shouted back, jumping with excitement.

'Comb your hair then,' Kisoo called after him. 'I don't want to go with a wild man.'

The clan had returned to their old village by this time.

'We'll make for the river,' Kisoo called as they set out half an hour later. 'There is a special tree that

Jon showed me. It is good for making bows. I think we will find some there.

'No, Kepa. Don't drink straight from the river,' he cautioned, as they reached the stream. 'Wait until you can find the good water for drinking, as you have been taught.' They stepped into the icy torrent to wash themselves, and then searched along the bank.

'Here it is! I've found it!' Kepa called. 'Look, a long leaf where the water is spouting out from the bank.'

'Come now, we'll try upstream,' called Kisoo when they had drunk, and led the way.

A kingfisher darted in front of them in jewelled flight.

There was the plop of a fish leaping after an insect and then a birdwing butterfly danced in front of them as if enticing them to follow.

'We'd best get on if you want your new bow,' Kisoo advised, but Kepa's attention had been caught by men's voices.

'They are building a bridge, Kisoo! Oh, please may we go and see?'

The boys made their way further upstream, and found men working from either side of the bank. They had already thrust stout poles into the water. Now, clinging to them, they were using their feet to bind vines on to further poles as an extension. At last they met in the middle of the torrent. The bridge was made.

'We did not often make bridges before,' Kisoo explained to his brother. 'We were too afraid of our enemies coming to attack us. But now everything is different. Jon says that since the government came and wrote names in its book, people have stopped killing. They are making this bridge so that someone will come and build a store. Then people will have the good things the white man brings.'

Seeing that he was absorbed, Kisoo slipped away. The next time Kepa looked up, his brother was beside him, his new bow nearly finished. The bridge was forgotten now.

'O Kisoo! Is it really for me?'

'Of course, little brother. Why, isn't it six dry seasons since you were born? Soon our mother will be telling you that you are too big to sleep with the women and will be sending you off to the man house. The bow you had is just a toy. This is a good strong one so that I can teach you to hunt.

'Come now,' he called, as he secured the last thong. 'Let us make our way up the mountain and you shall try it out. Once you are a good shot I will take you out on a night's hunting.'

But just then the older boy froze, silencing his brother by the merest gesture. The kingfisher had flashed again along their reach of the river and come to rest on the branch of a willow.

Kisoo made to fit an arrow to his bow but then became aware of his brother's unspoken plea. Not needing to speak assent, he handed him his own sharpened arrow.

Kepa's eye was true, his bow strong. The arrow sped on its way and before the beautiful creature was aware, the ecstasy of life was over.

'Careful, Kepa! Careful!' warned Kisoo as his brother stepped out into the water, for though the river was shallow, it was swift enough to carry a man away.

Clinging onto a branch, he took hold of Kepa's hand and held it tightly as the boy reached out and brought the bedraggled trophy to shore.

'Yallyee! Yallyee!' they laughed, dancing around and embracing each other. 'Kepa, you are going to be a mighty hunter.'

They made their way now to higher ground and sat down on a mound overlooking the valley. A few snow white clouds floated below them in a sea of blue.

'Pull them out carefully, Kepa,' Kisoo advised. 'The men will want these feathers when they decorate themselves for the tribal dance. They will pay you cowrie shells for them.

'There now, you collect some firewood and I will run and ask for fire from the house over there.'

Soon the sticks were crackling cheerfully as the

boys squatted, holding the tiny carcass over the flames.

'Tell me about the broken bow, Kisoo,' Kepa asked. He had heard it many times before, but a story could only mature with the telling.

'Was it really God who led you to that village, Kisoo?' he asked, when he had come to the end. 'Could he know about you and the shame you felt? Can God see us?'

'God knows each one of us,' Kisoo replied simply. 'He knows all about you, Kepa. He knows your name. He loves you.'

'Time to get the pigs in,' their mother called that evening. Nights were extra chilly in the dry season and they were all happy to go into the warmth. Kepa ran obediently to help. Once the sow was in the stall the piglets came squealing in around her.

'She is a wise one, the mother pig. She knows her own stall, but some of these young boars, they do not like to obey,' laughed his mother. She gave one a whack with her stick. 'There now, they are all in.'

The women and children squeezed past the stalls which were by the fire and moved towards their sleeping room at the back of the house.

'When I am big enough to go to the man house, I will be able to sleep by the fire,' Kepa complained, for the night was cold. He snuggled up to his mother for warmth.

'Do you think that we should sleep by the fire then and leave the pigs in the cold?' retorted his mother. 'If you want to be rich you must learn to care for the pigs, for they are our wealth.' But Kepa did not answer. He had enjoyed an exciting day, and as the warmth crept into his limbs he fell into a deep sleep.

Over in the man house some of the men were already on their beds, but though it was late, the boys were not yet willing to cover over the fire. They had been talking about the new bridge and one story had led to another.

Suddenly one of them lifted his finger. They were all alert then, straining to catch the sound he had heard. The next moment they were scrambling out through the low doorway.

'Fire! Fire!' they screamed. 'The woman house is on fire.'

They had realised that the crackling noise catching their attention was their dreaded enemy. A spark must have rested among the low rafters, and kindled into a blaze.

Hearing the roaring now, the women were struggling out past the pens. 'Ai! Ai! Ai!' they screamed in despair, while trying to drag out the frightened creatures. 'Help us! Help us!' The men rushed to the task, chopping away at the blazing thatch but the fire roared up into the darkness.

It was Kisoo who realised that his brother was missing. 'Kepa! Where is Kepa?' he cried in anguish, but his mother was struggling with the sow and had no other thought.

'Kepa!' again he cried, hoping that a little hand would appear from the dark shadows and thrust itself into his, but there was no answer. In torment he rushed to the back of the house. Was it possible that his brother had been left in the room there and was sleeping through all the commotion?

Wailing in his anguish, Kisoo seized an axe and began to hack through the flimsy walls of the house. With his bare hands he pulled away the already blazing grasses.

'Oh Jesus, help me,' he tried to cry, but fear was gripping his throat and no sound came out. Blinded by smoke, he groped his way along the floor until his hand touched a little body.

'Kepa! Kepa!' he screamed, dragging the child out through the wall of fire before he himself collapsed unconscious on the ground.

The pigs were all out, led away to a pen until they could make other arrangements for them.

The house had been left to its destruction, and in the light of the fire that was still raging they cut a bed of leaves and lay Kisoo on it.

The mother, nursing Kepa to her breast, squatted beside him. Trying to comfort one child, she mourned for the other.

'O Kisoo ee ee ee,' she sang in a woeful dirge.

'You brought God's book to us oo.

You loved your little brother oo.

Into the fire you went to save him.

Must you die to save you brother?

O Kisoo ee ee ee.'

From across the mountain they had seen the blaze. Now a cry rang out. 'What has happened? Are the pigs safe?'

'The pigs are safe, but Kisoo has died in the fire. Come for the purpose of crying.'

From mountain to mountain the call was passed on. 'Kisoo is dead oo! Come for the purpose of crying.'

The boy that lay on the bed of leaves was moaning. His lips moved but no one thought to get him water or to try to ease his pain.

'Come for the purpose of crying,' they called.

9

KISOO NEEDS HELP

Jon's breath came in gasps. He felt as if an iron band was around his chest; that his legs were weighted with stones. At last he gained the crest of the mountain, but his heart sank as he realised that yet another lay before him.

Sinking down on to a fallen log, he carefully snuffed out the smouldering embers of the torch of grasses that he had carried. He did not want to start another fire. Already there was a lightening of the eastern sky. A chirping from the bushes signalled to him that morning would soon be here.

'O Father God,' Jon prayed, though not aloud, for he was still struggling to get his breath, 'Let me be in time. Please let me be in time.' He rose, finding new strength and began to run through the gardens, down toward the river.

'Kisoo is dead oo! Come for the purpose of crying!' The call had echoed from mountain to mountain until at last it had reached Jon's village.

'Teacher Jon,' they had exclaimed, all talking at once, 'Is not this the boy who came to stay here among us? He was very careful to read God's book. Oh! That young boy! Ai! Ai! Ai!' and they sat down, wailing loudly.

A terrible fear had gripped Jon's heart, but then anger had blazed up to put this enemy to flight.

'Stop your crying!' he commanded. 'We don't even know if he is dead. For is not this the way of our people? One has only to break a leg and we start to dig his grave; but God is teaching us better ways. Listen!'

He had their attention now.

'I have told you how Kisoo came to me when I was staying in the village up on the ridge; how he had run away from his home and God led him to me.'

'Yes,' joined in Luka. 'The white man said he was a key, put into your hand so that you could open a door to that part of our tribe. You know *key*,' he explained, seeing that some of them did not understand, 'that small thing of iron that the white man uses to open a door that is fastened.' They were nodding now.

'That's right,' Jon said. 'But don't you see? If this boy dies the door may close again. So don't start crying! Pray! Pray that I will be able to get there in time, and that God will use me so that Kisoo's life will be saved.'

And so, while they had sat around their fires and prayed through the night, Jon had been hurrying through the mountains.

Kisoo still lay on his bed of leaves, moaning and twitching, with nothing to protect him from the cold night air. His people were squatting in a circle around him, their wailing cries rising and falling like the moaning of the wind through the casuarina trees.

'Kisoo saved his brother from the house fire oo!

He died to save his brother oo oo!'

Now and again a hysterical scream would rise from his mother as she reached out to touch her son. The child at her breast was sleeping through it all.

The circle of mourners was ever growing. As people reached the place for crying, they would daub their bodies with mud and add their voices to the lament.

'The teacher! Teacher Jon is coming!' It was only a whisper but the children, unable to bear the burden of grief, were glad of an excuse to get away. They ran down the hillside to welcome their friend and escort him to the village.

'Tell me what happened,' he commanded, with the little breath he had.

'The woman house caught fire. Kepa was still

asleep and was left in the house, and Kisoo broke through the walls to carry him out. Yes, Kepa is unhurt, but Kisoo! Ai! Ai!' and they added their little voices to the lament, as they had been taught.

Jon, his strength regained now, strode into the circle of mourners. A swift glance assured him that he was in time and yet his heart contracted with fear as he saw the sorry state of the one who had become like a son to him.

'Silence!' he commanded. 'Stop your crying!' Some of the men stood up to remonstrate, but then cowered down before the fierceness of his anger.

'Why are you crying, like heathen people, instead of praying as I have taught you?' he demanded. 'You are weeping and wailing as if there were no God in heaven! Did you not promise to listen to God's word; to walk in his road? Why, Kisoo learned to read God's book so that he could read it to you - but have you been listening?'

Their eyes were downcast. Jon could see that he had struck the right note.

'Come now!' His tone was softer. 'Let us ask God to forgive us. And then we can pray for Kisoo's life to be spared.'

And so it was that when the sun finally peeped over the mountain it found a company of people on their knees. And even as they felt the early rays warming their chilled bodies, so the warmth of hope was creeping into their hearts.

Jon stood again, his face stern, for it was a hard thing he was about to ask of them.

'I believe God has heard our prayer and will save Kisoo. But we must do our part. You know that God has sent the white man to our land to help us. They have brought us God's book and they have also brought us their medicine. I feel in my heart that Kisoo won't get better without this medicine. There is a doctor on the other side of the mountain, across the new bridge,' he told them. One or two nodded. They had heard of this place. There was a store there. 'We must take Kisoo there very quickly.'

There was a stir now among the people. Talk flowed to and fro. If there was hope of someone's recovery then they should sacrifice pigs to appease the bad spirits that were attacking that person; but as far as Kisoo was concerned there had seemed no point in wasting their precious pigs. But to carry a dying boy all that way for white man's medicine. This was something new.

Jon walked to the edge of the clearing while they were discussing the issue. 'Lord Jesus!' he murmured, 'Lord Jesus!' Somehow he couldn't find any other words to express his prayer. He knew that it was not just Kisoo's life he was fighting for, but somehow it was the life of these people as well.

He turned in time to see some of the young men

leave the clearing and run off into the forest. Had they been sent to dig the grave? Jon was almost ready to daub his own body with mud to express his grief, but then he heard the ring of axes. This was not digging. They were cutting branches to make a stretcher. 'Thank you, Lord Jesus, thank you,' whispered Jon.

'Yes, we will take him to the doctor,' Andupi declared as Jon returned among them. 'I myself will go to care for him.' He had already sent the women running to their gardens to fetch food for the journey.

'Father, I come? I help you look after Kisoo?' Andupi felt a little hand tugging at his and looked down into Kepa's pleading eyes. It was a marvel to him that his child was unharmed after the ordeal. 'Yes, my son, you shall come too.'

Maybe he would have to carry the boy some of the way, but he knew that Kepa, of all people would be able to help his brother.

Jon did not start out immediately after the stretcher-bearing party. 'No,' he called to the mourners, 'it isn't time to go to your homes. You must stay here and pray.'

As he left them and ran to catch up with the bearers, he realised how fragile life could be. Even now he knew that only by a miracle could the white man's medicine save him.

How fragile too was the spiritual life of these people. How quickly they had turned back to their old ways. The birds of the air had come to snatch away the seed of God's word that he had planted. And now it seemed almost as if the destiny of these people hung on the slender thread of the life of this one lad. Could it be that God would answer their prayers?

10

MONDO IS AFRAID

'Look! The sun is coming out!' The girls came tumbling out of the house to enjoy its warmth. Mondo couldn't see the golden light as it painted the mountain peaks in tips of fire but could feel its comfort. She soon found herself a grassy place to sit, and deftly swept the ground clean. Though blind, she knew that the pigs left their traces everywhere.

'Ayuna! Come for the purpose of getting lice from my hair,' Yayowana called. Ayuna ran willingly. There was comfort in the companionship of helping each other in this way. Soon the girls were seated in a circle, each busily searching the head of the one in front.

Mondo sat apart, listening to their chatter, and the occasional crunch which told her that there remained one less of the unwanted guests. She wasn't able to search, and so must be content to scratch her own infested head.

She struggled with the bark that she was rubbing and twisting to make into string. She still had not mastered the art of crocheting and would have to learn. Mondo would have to prove her usefulness, or she would be cast out, abandoned. These hardy highlanders had no time for passengers.

'Lord Jesus, help me,' Mondo whispered, as she patiently twisted the fibre. The old one would help her for becoming feeble herself, she had a fellow feeling for the blind girl; but the women had stayed in their garden shelter when the rain came, and doubtless they were digging away again by now.

Mondo was learning to call upon the name of the Lord. She had missed Kisoo and his Bible reading since the house fire. She missed little Kepa too. She would never forget how he had helped her to cross the log bridge.

'Fear is darkness, Mondo,' he had told her. 'The Lord Jesus wants to chase the fear out of our hearts. Ask him, Mondo! You ask him!'

She remembered the day he had run up to her, his excitement bubbling over. 'I did it, Mondo! I did it!'

'Did what, Kepa?' She was impatient. It is easy to do anything if you can see.

'I crossed the log bridge with my eyes closed.'

Mondo was touched. She felt the hot tears trying to burst from her sightless eyes. She spoke roughly, to hide her feelings. 'What a stupid thing to do,

Kepa. You might have been killed.'

'No - it's easy, Mondo. I practised first on a log on the ground. You can feel with your toes. And I asked Jesus to help me. I'm only a little boy and he helped me. You are bigger than I am, Mondo, so I know he will help you too.'

When at last the time had come for them to return to their other gardens, Mondo had known that inevitably they must reach the dreaded river. She hadn't forgotten how Kepa, his eyes closed, walked across the log while the river raged below. His very presence had been an unspoken plea to her to let Jesus chase the fear away.

Their houses had been boarded up, the net bags loaded and they had set out on their journey. The fear had gripped at her throat, clutching her stomach. 'I could wade through the river again,' she had thought. 'Perhaps the current won't be so strong this time,' but just then Andupi's brother had come up to her.

'No risking the lives of our girls by asking them to wade with you through the river, Mondo. You would all be carried away.'

'Here! Take Mondo's net bag for her,' Kainowana had commanded as they reached the bridge. 'Now! Give me your hand!' Mondo had trembled. She remembered that she had not dared refuse, or she might have found herself left behind, abandoned.

'You can do it, Mondo! You can do it!' Kepa had called. 'Jesus will help you.'

'Good friend Jesus,' she had whispered, and had then felt her feet secure on the wood beneath her. The river had no longer seemed threatening as step by step, she had made her way across. The girls had applauded as she safely reached the other side. Truly Jesus had chased away the darkness of fear.

She was longing for Kepa to return. Somehow he gave her courage for living. Andupi had brought them news that Kisoo was alive and getting stronger, but it was two moons now since he had gone. Surely they would be back soon.

As she sat, Mondo suddenly became aware that she was alone. Like a flock of tiny birds that would rise from the bushes and whirr away into the sky, so the girls had scampered off. What was it that had caught their attention? Nothing fearsome, or she would have heard their screams. Perhaps they had glimpsed some beautiful bird or butterfly; or had they heard something that she hadn't? She strained her ears to listen. The men had left home on a hunting expedition the previous night, and were not home yet. Had they decided to go and meet them?

Mondo felt desolate, forsaken. Surely they could have spared a thought to tell her where they were going. Didn't they know that she was alone? She started, hearing a scuffle close beside her, then she relaxed. It was surely only one of the pigs. But then a twig snapped. She was shaking now. Should she go into the house? But that was no protection from an arrow, or a snake. 'No, no, sit still,' she thought, 'I am only imagining things.'

'Oo oo oo!' she sang out. 'Where are you oo?' She thought she heard laughter from the direction of the river, but there was no answering 'Oo!' except for a faint echo.

'Oh well,' I'll just sit here and wait,' she thought. 'They'll come back soon enough. And the women will be returning. They'll be gathering the pigs in.'

She took up her task again, struggling with the unwilling string, humming a little tune to convince herself that she was not afraid. But the warmth of the sun could not prevent her limbs from trembling, and her ears seemed to be outstretched for the least sound. Again she heard the snap of a twig, then there came the faintest rustling in the bushes. Her nose wrinkled at the unpleasant odour of a stink bug. Something or someone had disturbed it.

Mondo stood up. It was more than lice that was causing the crawling sensation in her hair. 'Who is there?' she called, but no one answered. She couldn't stay there on her own and wait for some enemy to come upon her. Was it some wild animal waiting to pounce upon her, or an evil spirit that had come to torment her ? Could it be - dread thought - an enemy come to 'pay back' a wrong, taking his spite on a defenceless blind girl while the rest of the clan was away?

'No good sitting here with my imaginings,' she muttered to herself, 'I'll go and find the girls.' Grasping her stick, she felt her way along the path. 'I am coming, too!' She tried to sing out boldly, but fear was gripping her throat and her voice came out as no more than a squeak.

A sudden wind whipped up, whirling around Mondo, snatching away any sound that might have carried down to the valley. Buffeted and bewildered, she was not sure now which direction they had taken, or even where she herself had come from.

At last the wind died down and in the distance the babble of the river could be heard once more. If she could make it there, she might regain her sense of direction. Slipping and sliding, sobbing and sighing, she struggled on. Surely relief must come. Someone would think of her and turn back to help her.

It was then that she heard the voice. 'Over here, Blind one! Are you looking for the girls? They have gone this way.'

Mondo didn't recognise the voice, but was grateful for any help. Cautiously, feeling the way with her stick, she stepped forward.

'That's it! Come!' again he called. 'They have

crossed to the other side. They are waiting for you. The water is shallow. There is no danger. I am coming across to meet you. Come!'

Hesitantly Mondo stepped into the icy stream. The water rushed against her legs. How could she know that she could trust this stranger? And yet why should she doubt him? And who else was there to help her? If he had wanted to kill her he could have leapt on her with his axe or killing stick while she had sat alone by the woman house. Surely he wouldn't make sport of her, luring her to her death?

'Come!' the voice called again. Once more she stepped forward. The coldness of the water was taking her breath, but the chill was gripping her heart too. 'I ... I am afraid,' she gasped, and then she remembered little Kepa. 'Fear is darkness, Mondo,' he had said. 'Ask Jesus to take the fear away.'

'Good friend Jesus!' she whispered. Why hadn't she remembered to call on him before? 'Jesus!' Strength was coming to her until at last it came out as a confident shout.

A sudden rush of the current caught her, and as she struggled to find her footing her stick swung round and struck against a rock. Mondo stumbled forward, only to find that she had turned full circle and was stepping up on to the bank.

'No! No! Not that way!' the voice called, but it's coaxing softness had gone. There was anger in it.

Surely, thought Mondo, it is an enemy who is on the opposite bank, trying to lure me to my death. And she was vulnerable. If he didn't succeed he could find another way to kill her. How could she hide from him? She didn't even know which way to run for safety. But she did know now that she was not alone, for the good friend Jesus had surely heard her cry. He wouldn't leave her. Surely, surely he would send help to save her from the enemy.

11

MONDO IS FOUND

The girls had not intended to leave Mondo on her own. It was just that they had forgotten about her. It was Popotanda who had first caught a glimpse of the bird of paradise. Lifting her head from the task of pest control, she had caught just a glimpse of the beautiful long tail feathers among the branches of the yar trees.

Following the leader, each head in turn was raised, and seeing a finger placed to her lips, they had tip-toed after the girl. There was little satisfaction in just beholding the sight. Such beauty must be displayed, and their purpose was either to capture or kill the poor creature.

It seemed as if the bird was making sport of them, for it flitted from tree to tree, leading them deeper into the forest. At last they stopped bewildered.

'Where did it go?' asked Popotanda, for there was no sign or sound of it.

'And where are we? Where do we go?' They

gazed at each other, a little afraid.

'No matter.' Tanowana tried to sound confident. 'We'll climb up to some open ground, and sing out. The women may hear us.' Scrambling up through the dense bush, they reached a more open hillock.

'Where are you, oo oo oo?' Their voices echoed out across the hills. They waited, listening, hoping for an answering cry. Far away they thought they heard the shrilling of women's voices and yet no one called out in response.

'Where are you, oo oo oo?' They joined in unison this time. Again the call rang out, but though they waited long there was no answer.

'There were voices in that direction,' Popotanda pointed with her nose. 'Perhaps they are quarrelling about something and are too busy to answer. Come, let's go. We are sure to find them.'

Scrambling and sliding down some loose shale searching for familiar landmarks, they made their way in the direction of the voices. Popotanda was still in the lead, but suddenly she turned back, huddling in amongst the others. 'What is it?' one began to ask, but then they all heard it. There was a crashing in the bushes. Something was coming their way. What could it be? Had they disturbed some wild pig who thought they were threatening her piglets? A cassowary maybe? But they had not knowingly intruded upon them or caused them any threat. Why should they attack them? It could not be an enemy for they had not heard the beating of drums or the rhythmic chanting that indicated trouble.

Just then the girls gave a little scream and clung to each other. The bushes parted right before them and then they began to laugh with relief. 'Kutuma!' they exclaimed. 'Aipi!' At once their shrill voices were raised, bombarding the boys with questions.

'We didn't know you were back. Did you catch a cassowary? Why didn't you answer when we called out?'

But fiercely the boys cautioned them to silence. 'Be quiet! You are in danger! Now, follow us silently! Not a sound.'

Trembling and wondering, the girls obediently followed Kutuma while a watchful Aipi took up the rear, his bow at the ready.

They had reached the safety of the village and found the women and little ones already there. While some of the young warriors stood on guard behind the sentinel trees now, they could relax and hear the story.

'Oh! Oh! Fine cassowary! Oh! We'll have a feast! Oh! You have done well! You have done well!' the girls exclaimed as they saw the body of the great ostrich-like bird,. They were prized, not only for their meat, but also for the claws which were used for making their killing sticks; and of course the feathers would make excellent adornment.

'And look! Look! Two chicks!' Little Losa pointed to the place where a pen was being erected. 'More good meat when they grow up.'

'And don't you go near them,' her mother warned. 'They are very fierce, even if they are small. It won't be long and they will be able to tear you open with one blow of their claws.'

'But what is the danger?' The girls were still mystified, and at last quietened down and were ready to listen.

'A mad man! One of Yapisa's line.'

Yapisa! Dread name, for that was the clan that Andupi had attacked.

'Some men met us on our way back from the hunt. We were making our way home happily and looking forward to the feast, when they found us. They told us he was heading this way. He probably knew our men were away on a hunt and thought he would get an easy victim for a pay back killing.

'An easy victim!' It was not until then that they remembered Mondo. Mondo! Where was she? It was as though they all thought of her at once. 'Ai! Ai! Ai!' the girls wailed, realising that they were being blamed. 'Ai! Poor Mondo! They have killed her! Ai! Ai!'

But while the women with their fatalistic attitude

joined in the weeping and wailing, the men were more practical. Directing two to stay on guard, they ran off in search of the blind girl. The honour of their clan was at stake, and they could not allow a mad man to gain a victory over them.

At last Leme's voice was heard, ringing out. 'Here she is! Down by the river! I have found her!' and then they were all gathering around her.

Mondo stretched out her hands in welcome. She didn't know whether to laugh or cry. 'He was there! There!' she told them. She pointed to where she had heard the stranger calling her, but now there was neither sight or sound of him. The men hunted long, but at length they returned to the village. Now they could concentrate on the task of preparing the feast.

Early next morning the fires were lit. While the stones were heated the pit was dug and at last the great bird, packed round with vegetables, was sealed in the earth oven. By evening it was ready.

Once they had all eaten and were content, it was time for telling stories. But it was not one of the old men's stories of long long ago. They told the story of a blind girl, and how that good friend Jesus had saved her from the enemy.

'Tell me, Mondo! Tell me again,' begged little Kepa, when he was home with Kisoo from the hospital, just a few days later.

'Jesus saved you, didn't he?' he commented,

satisfied, when she had come to the end of her story once again.

Kepa had stories to tell too, many stories. Two moons had passed since they had carried Kisoo to the hospital, and his eyes and ears had been open to all that had gone on around him. He wasn't old enough to tell his stories when the men were present, but he told them in the woman house, and Mondo was always a ready listener.

One day he told her, 'Mondo, there was a woman who came to the hospital with bad eyes. The doctor put medicine in them and said it would make them better. If you went to the hospital, Mondo, they might make your eyes better.'

The girl sat silently, and so the child persisted. 'Jesus took the darkness of fear from your heart. Couldn't he take the darkness from your eyes?'

But Mondo still had a lot of fear in her heart. Yes, truly, her good friend Jesus had helped her to cross the log bridge. Yes, he had saved her when left all alone, an enemy had sought to lure her to her death. He had sent the young men at just the right time. But to leave her clan and go on a long journey amongst an unknown people! This was asking too much. Mondo didn't want to hear about it.

She left the comfort of the fire and went outside into the mist of clouds that were wrapping themselves around the little village.

12

KEPA HELPS KISOO

Kisoo sat resting against one of the great trees that stood sentinel around his village home. Far below, he could see the women digging in their gardens. They would be filling their net bags with sweet potato for the meal that evening. Now and again a shrill voice would ring out as they called one of the children to them. Away to the side he heard an occasional shout from where the men were working to build a new house.

Men! Some of his own brothers were included among the men now, for had they not been away in the bush for their initiation ceremonies while he had been in the hospital? And all the dancing and celebration; it was all over and he had not been included.

He had stood and watched them working for a while. The poles of the roof were all firmly attached to the king post, and now they were interlacing them with branches. They would soon be ready for the thatching. The boys had already been sent off to fetch the long grass that they used.

But he couldn't stay standing for long. He still felt weak and ill, and in any case it was awful watching them all working so happily together when he could do nothing.

'Everyone is involved,' he sighed, 'except me. I am useless.' He looked at his hands, twisted and scarred. Even holding them up to look at them seemed to bring on the pain. He tucked them away under his arms, out of sight.

'Yes, they gave white man's medicine to save my life, but what use is it if I cannot use my hands? I might as well be dead,' he grumbled to himself, although in his heart of hearts he knew that this was not true.

Kisoo did not remember much of the night of the fire. He could still recall the terrible fear on realising that his little brother was inside the burning house. 'Kepa! Kepa!' he had cried out many times from his bed in the clinic, and then from far away he would hear a little voice, 'Kisoo! Kisoo! It is alright. I am here. You saved me, Kisoo!'

Then he would sink back into a deep pit of darkness where he was struggling, struggling. At one time it was as though he was falling down, down, down; until, from somewhere far above him he heard voices: 'Lord Jesus, we claim this boy for you.' And he had felt himself being pulled into the air and into the light.

Many times again he had felt himself sinking. He did not know that Jon, and the other Christians had wrestled in prayer; but he did remember that whenever he had called out, little Kepa had been there. He could recall how once, when the pain was very bad he had sung to him his favourite song, 'That good friend Jesus.'

Kisoo looked up. He could hear the low chanting of the boys as they returned from the forest. Grass covered their heads so that they looked like walking gardens.

'Even Kepa is too busy to think of me now,' he complained. But he had misjudged the lad, for seeing his big brother sitting so forlornly, he had dumped his load and run quickly up to him. They had always been close as brothers, but since Kisoo had saved him from the fire Kepa had become more than ever his devoted servant.

'I have come from helping with the new house,' Kepa volunteered, though Kisoo hadn't acknowledged his presence.

'Shall I go to fetch you water?' Kisoo gave the merest shake of his head. Kepa felt hurt and rebuffed. He wanted to run back and join in the fun of the house building, but he wouldn't give up. There must be something he could do to shake his brother out of this depression. Then he had an idea. Jumping up, he ran towards the man house.

'Even he won't stay with me,' sighed Kisoo, full of self pity, but the next moment the boy was back, with something in his hand.

'My Bible! Why, I had forgotten all about it,' thought Kisoo, but he did not say it out loud. He kept his hands tucked under his arms. 'How can I read now?' was all he said.

'I'll help you, Kisoo.' Kepa had the persistence of a doctor. He was determined to see his patient improve. He pulled his brother's legs down so that he could place the book open on his knees. Then, opening it, he took a long leaf and placed it under the words as he had seen the older boy do. 'Read it to me,' he commanded. Obediently, Kisoo began.

'*Listen!* he read. *Once there was a man who went out to plant corn*. Why, this is the story that Jon told us in church,' he exclaimed.

It was the story that had had made him recognise the need to have a Bible and read it for himself. He read on, sounding out the words, and as he read, his depression began to slip away. He nodded to Kepa to close the book, watching as the boy carefully wrapped it up again.

'Why, it is no wonder I have been feeling miserable,' he exclaimed. 'I had forgotten all about reading God's book.' He sat quietly for a while, then went on, 'Do you remember how, in the clinic, you coaxed me when I didn't want to eat.'

Kepa nodded. 'I remember. Once you started to eat you began to grow strong,' he affirmed.

'And now you are having to coax me to read God's word. This is food for us too. Only if we read it every day we will get strong in our spirits. You have done well, little brother.'

'I will help you, Kisoo. We will read it every day?' There was pleading in his eyes.

'We will read it every day,' was the response. Kepa was content. He ran to put the book back in its safe place then returned, hesitating before asking, 'I go to help with the house?' He was longing to go, but wouldn't leave his brother unless he was willing.

'Yes, you go, Kepa. I will come and watch.'

And so, every morning Kepa would bring the Bible. Finding a sunny spot, Kisoo would read while his brother held the leaf as a marker. Always after reading, he would question Kepa to see if he too had understood, and then they would pray. One morning, as they turned the page, Kepa's attention was diverted by the picture that was on the far side.

'What is that?' he asked.

'Why, that is a dumb man. Jesus is putting a finger on his tongue so that he will be able to talk.'

'And will he be able to talk?'

'Of course he will.'

'Why did Jesus do that?' Kepa persisted.

'Why? Because they asked him. Come, Kepa. I'll read the story to you.'

Kepa was listening intently.

'Kisoo?' he asked again. 'If Jesus made that man's ears better because they asked him, why can't we ask him to make your hands better?'

Kisoo was silent. He had been so helpless and miserable because of the pain in his hands and had not even thought to ask his 'good friend Jesus'. 'We can ask him, Kepa,' he said simply. 'Come, we'll go into the church now and pray.

'Lord Jesus,' Kisoo prayed when they had knelt down, 'Thank you for making me strong to save Kepa from the house fire, and thank you for sending Jon to take me to the hospital so that I did not die. But, Lord Jesus, you know that my hands pain me so much and I cannot use them. Please heal my hands like you healed the ears of the deaf boy. Amen.'

'Amen,' echoed Kepa. He was satisfied now. 'I'm going hunting with my new bow,' he called, and ran off into the sunshine.

Every morning Kepa would bring the Bible and every morning they would open this precious book together. Kepa was not only holding the marker now. He was becoming interested in the shape of the words and the letters.

'What does this one say?' he asked one morning. 'It is like a man with his arms sticking out.'

'Why, that is letter K. It is in your name, Kepa, and mine - Kisoo. Look, I'll show you and you can write it.'

He smoothed the earth with his foot, took a stick in his hand and began to write, 'Ka - ke - ki' - then he stopped and looked at the stick. He looked at his brother. Kepa's big brown eyes were opened wide.

'Your hands, Kisoo!' at last he exclaimed, 'You are holding the stick!'

'Yes, my hands! They aren't paining me! They aren't paining me! Why, Kepa, where are you going?' for Kepa was pulling him to his feet.

'To the church of course. We must say thank you to Jesus.'

As Kisoo knelt there in the church he remembered the time he had first heard the children singing, 'That good friend Jesus.' What a good friend indeed he had become to him. Now that his hands were better, was it possible that in some way he could be a friend to Jesus; that there was some work he could do for him?

13

MONDO SHOWS THE WAY

The strange thing was that, even though Mondo couldn't see to read, she had been the reason for the literacy class starting.

'Kepa! Kepa-o!' Yayowana had called one morning, as the women and girls were making their way to their gardens.

'No, don't call him,' said his mother, 'for he is with Kisoo, helping him to read God's book.'

'Helping him,' laughed the girl. 'He is learning to read it himself. He even knows how to write some of the letters.'

'Yes, he's shown me,' joined in Popotanda.

Once Mondo knew that Kisoo was reading from the book, she refused to go on with the women. 'Ai! Ai! Ai!' she wailed, 'I want to go and hear God's book'

'Be quiet! Come! We have to go and dig our gardens!' They tried to drag her along with them, but Mondo was not to be moved. She stood her ground and continued to wail until for the sake of peace, Popotanda was assigned to lead her back to the village.

That evening Popotanda, too, was full of the reading lesson. 'Look! I can write P for Popotanda,' and she took a stick and wrote it on the ground. Now the other children were envious, and the parents too.

'When we go into God's house and Jon reads to us from the Bible, then there is light,' said one of the men, 'but when he has gone, our hearts are dark. If we too can learn to read, we can each have our own book.'

They sat outside on the grass, talking long and loud. Each one had to have his say, and they were so engrossed that the night crept up unawares. The darkness could not extinguish the flame that had been kindled there in that highland village, for the decision had been made.

The elders would speak to Jon about their having literacy classes. And of course, there was no dispute about who should be their teacher. Kisoo, was already acknowledged as a reader. He would be the teacher.

'Mondo, it was Jesus who took the pain out of Kisoo's hands. I know he can put the light back in your eyes if we ask him,' pressed little Kepa one evening, as they sat by the fire in the woman house.

'Yes, I know he can, Kepa. And I do ask him. Every night I ask him. But - not to go to the hospital. I have fear in my heart to go all that way, and among strange people. Please don't speak of it, Kepa. I don't want to hear about it.'

So Kepa didn't speak of it again, not to her, though that didn't stop him praying about it. When he learned that some of them were planning to work on the road that the government was building, he was amazed to hear that Mondo was to be among the party.

'When we work to make the road, the government men will pay us. Then we will have money to buy our own books. Don't you know that Jon is going to bring us special books so that Kisoo can teach us to read and write?' she told them. 'And then we must each have our own Bible.'

'But Mondo!' the women reasoned, 'You can't see to read and write. And besides, we have to cross the vine bridge, where the river is very wide. You will be afraid. Why don't you stay here with the old ones. Someone has to look after the pigs and the children.'

But Mondo was determined. She wanted her own book.

'If I have my own book I will sleep with my head on it. Then its words can go into my mind. And I can ask people to read it to me any time I want. Besides, money is good. There is a store there at the other side of the river. I will buy soap, and a good spade for digging the garden, and a blouse to wear when I go to church.'

'Yes, yes,' the others joined in, 'and buckets, so that we can carry much water, not just the little we can get in a gourd; and a wonderful thing called a lamp, with a tiny fire in it, so that we can see, even in the night.'

And so it was that, when a group of them left their village high up on the mountain, Mondo was among them.

She was trailing behind as usual, holding someone's hand, or when the path was too narrow, a stick that one of the girls held out for her.

They climbed down towards the river and when at last they caught a glimpse of the vine bridge, this time it was not only Mondo who was afraid.

The young men had already crossed, for though afraid, they were ashamed to show it. They had run on ahead to make sure of getting work.

The women, however, were sitting on the bank, watching the bridge swinging and swaying.

'No! No! Let's go back,' said one. 'It is too dangerous.' They sat, their arms wrapped around their necks, trembling with fear rather than with cold.

'Kainiona! If you will go first, then we will follow,' suggested one.

'Oh no! You go first!'

And so it went on.

Mondo sat silently where she had been left. Surely, after coming all this way, they could not turn back now.

If only little Kepa were there. He was always so quick to comfort and support her, and somehow she felt that if he would go before her she would have had courage to go across. But the little children had not been allowed to come, and in any case he would not have left Kisoo.

She remembered her fear when they had needed to cross the log bridge, and how the little fellow had crossed with his eyes closed, in order to give her confidence.

Slowly, the blind girl stood up. 'Here! Come for the purpose of leading me to the bridge,' she commanded.

'Ei! Ei!' the others responded, as one obediently walked with her down the bank. Mondo placed her feet on the poles that stretched over the bank and put her hand on the beginning of the slender rail.

'Lord Jesus,' Mondo prayed, 'Kepa isn't here, but you are here. Please take me safely over this bridge.'

Cautiously, inch by inch, she stepped out, conscious of the chattering anxiety of the girls behind her. She moved a few yards and then froze as she felt the slender support swaying beneath her. The river gurgled and growled angrily, rushing on its way below.

'Oh! Oh! I'm coming back!' she cried in terror. 'I can't go on!' but she found it was impossible for her to turn.

'You can do it, Mondo, I know you can.'

It was not the women, but it was Kepa's voice that came to her; Kepa, who had never given up praying for her. She took one more step, then another. She knew she must be nearing the other side, for she was climbing upward now. She could hear the women gasp as she bent down, seeking to find the hand rail, but there was nothing now to hold on to on the one side.

'You are nearly there, Mondo. Two more steps.' The voice did not come from behind, but in front. It was Kakiama.

Andupi had sent some of the boys back to see that the women made it across the river. Encouraged by his voice, Mondo stretched out one hand towards him, sliding her grip along on the right side. She eased her feet forward until, beyond the poles of the bridge, she found soft mud. Rolling down, she lay panting on the ground.

One by one, amidst shrieks of fear and excitement, the women and girls joined her. 'Well done! Well done Mondo!'

How proud and happy she felt. She, who was always made to feel a burden, had helped them in their time of need.

Reaching their destination, there was excitement now as they mixed with other clans; people they only saw when they had their great pig feasts, or when they went to war.

Now they were all working happily side by side. Some were digging out the ground from the hill side, others breaking stones, while the younger ones carried them down to make the road surface. Some government men were organising them, and at last they began to see the road winding its way up over the range.

Mondo couldn't see the goods arrayed in the little store, but she liked to go there with the others and hear the wonders described to her. 'Matches? What is that?' she exclaimed in fear and wonder, as she heard the quick *zip* and heard the gush of the flame, feeling its heat.

When the man came to pay them, now it was time to decide. What would they buy with these wonderful stones they called money?

Some of the women bought brightly coloured string to make their net bags, but this was not of interest to a blind girl. She was happy to have a spade for the garden, though. How much better than the digging sticks they had used through the centuries, and she too wanted a blouse and a towel.

'But make sure you have enough money left to pay for our books,' she cautioned the others.

They were on their way home now when suddenly their happiness was turned to sadness. They had reached as far as the vine bridge when they realised that the young men were not with them.

'Have they gone on ahead of us?' asked Popotanda.

'Call out! Perhaps they are still coming,' suggested Wakenona, but Andupi shook his head, and now they could see that his eyes were filled with pain.

'It is no use calling out,' he told them. 'They won't hear, and even if they did, they won't come.'

He went on to tell them the sad news.

'Some men came to the man house last night and promised them plenty of money. He promised them tobacco and strong drink and all the good things the white man has if they would go with them to work in a far away place.

'We pleaded with them not to go, for what will happen to our people with our young men gone? But it was no use. They set off, many of them, very early this morning. They were walking over the range to a place where some trucks were waiting for them.

'But come! We must go home!' he commanded,

seeing that the women were about to set up a wailing. 'The others will be waiting for us.'

Sadly, one by one, the men taking the lead, they crossed the bridge which had held such terrors for them. But the women did not need Mondo to set them an example this time. Home was on the other side, and soon they were calling out and there were the children skipping down the mountain side to greet them.

But how could they tell them the sad news? And how could they dispel the fear that it was not only good that the white man had brought them?

14

THE NEW TEACHER

Kisoo awoke with a start in the man house, his heart contracting at the sound of the crackling fire. But then he drew a deep breath and relaxed, driving away the fear.

This was a very special day of celebration; for was not this the day the white man was coming to their village? Away in the distance he could hear the squealing of the pigs that were to be slaughtered. His mouth watered at the prospect of meat. The crackling had come from the fires they were lighting for the earth oven. This would be a feast indeed.

'Bring more wood,' Kisoo ordered, as he went outside to help to supervise the work. 'The fire is not hot enough yet.'

The children scurried to obey their teacher. Carefully they had placed the stones into the flames and were now adding sticks. Some of the boys were digging a large pit, while the girls were coming with armfuls of green leaves from the tea plant.

There came a chanting from the hill-side below, and soon the men appeared carrying the portions of meat. Women and children were coming from far and wide with offerings of food from their gardens.

'Carefully now! Here! Use this wood as tongs! Place the stones in the pit!' It was Andupi, Kisoo's father who had taken command now. 'There now, cover the stones with leaves.'

They were crowding around each other as each wanted to place his own contribution in the earth oven. At last it was all inside. Leaves were laid to cover the food and more heated stones. The men took over now, covering the hole with earth until there was only a slight rise to show that the oven was there.

Kisoo, meanwhile, already washed and wearing the new shorts his father had brought him, was waiting at the edge of the clearing. He was straining his ears for the call signalling that Jon and the white man were on their way.

He called Kepa, 'Go down to the river. Here, I'll give you my soap. Take all the children with you and see that they wash well. We don't want any dirty boys or girls going to meet the visitor.'

He could hear the excited laughter and chatter as they scampered down the mountainside. Truly, today was a very special day. But he was still at his watch when they returned with bodies glistening and teeth chattering.

'Go and stand in the sunshine, over by the man house,' he advised. 'You'll soon be warm. I'll call you as soon as he is coming. He surely won't be long now.'

There was a soft rustling behind him and Kisoo turned to see Yayowana resplendent in a new grass skirt. 'Will the white man like me?' she asked.

'We all like you,' was his response. 'You look fine.'

He felt his heart swelling with pride as he looked round at the people gathering on the open ground around the church. How different their lives had become since Teacher Jon had come to teach them from God's book.

'Can't we go and meet them?' the children pleaded, impatiently.

'Jon promised to call us when they reached that mountain,' Kisoo replied. 'We must wait. Don't go away though,' he warned, seeing them gather around Leme for a game of marbles. But as time went on others too were getting restless.

'We might as well go to our gardens,' suggested one of the women. 'The food won't be ready until the evening. We can be back in time for the feast.'

'Ask them to wait,' Kisoo begged his father. 'The white man will come. I know he will. Jon promised.'

'Yes, he promised. But anything could have

happened. You know that the white man has to come part of the way in his machine on the new road. But last week there was a very heavy rain, remember. There may have been a landslide and perhaps the road has washed away.'

'Yes, or the bridge may have broken and they don't have enough men to fix it,' added another of the men.

Fear was crawling up around Kisoo's heart, gripping, choking him. This was to have been such a special day. He had worked so hard in preparation, ever since Jon had told him.

He turned away, choking back his tears; and then suddenly he realised - 'Lord Jesus,' he prayed, 'it wasn't only for the white man that we have been preparing. It was for you. And you are here. You will never disappoint us or let us down.'

He strode into the middle of the clearing and spoke with authority.

'Listen!' he said. 'Blow on the conch shell again, for in a few minutes we are going to start church. Today is a special day of thanksgiving. Yes, we had hoped to welcome the white man and to thank him for writing God's word for us in our language. But if he doesn't come, we must still give thanks to God. He is here with us, so let us go into the church and begin our service.'

'But the teacher isn't here,' one began to complain, but another silenced him. 'Isn't Kisoo our teacher now?'

And so the call wailed out far over the mountains and Jon and Karl, struggling up a steep incline, heard it and quickened their steps.

'I was afraid we would have been too late, with the jeep breaking down,' confessed Karl, 'I thought we might have arrived to find they had all gone home. And this is the only chance I will have to visit these people before I leave for Australia.'

'Yes, truly,' said Jon. 'I had so much wanted you to see the difference that God's word has made to the villagers. Especially since Kisoo has been teaching them to read.'

As they drew nearer, one or two little faces began to peep at them from the bushes.

'Where are the other children?' Jon asked.

'They are listening to the good talk,' was the answer. Jon turned to look at Karl. Had they indeed started the service? His heart quickened. He had so many villages to reach and it had seemed such an impossible task to give them the teaching that they needed. Could it be that God was raising up some-one to share the task with him?

'No! No! Don't call out to say that we are coming,' they cautioned the children. 'We don't want to disturb the service. We will surprise them.'

Once they had reached the church, the two men

stood quietly for a few moments, unobserved, a hymn of thanksgiving rising silently from their hearts; for Kisoo was standing at the front, telling his favourite story of the sower. He went on to tell of his desire that God's word should grow in his own heart, and of how Kepa had brought the book for him to read when he was recovering from his burns.

'And then Teacher Jon brought me books that the white man had written, and the village elders asked me to teach my people. Today I have asked some of those in the class to read to you from God's book.'

Kepa was the first one out. 'Jesus began to teach by Lake Galilee...' he began. Kisoo took the book from him as he finished his passage and Leme continued.

Then Kokame came and read. She was an old woman, but she had been hungry for God's word. She read her verse.

Next Mondo, the blind girl, came out, Kepa proudly leading her. 'She cannot read,' Kisoo explained, 'but she has learned God's word.' She said her verse too.

Karl and Jon had joined them now. After the excitement had subsided and they had sung and prayed, Karl spoke to them.

'When I came to your country,' he told them, 'it was very hard for me to learn your language. It was very hard to write God's book so that you could understand, and even harder to find people who wanted to listen and learn and obey this word. But now truly I understand that God's word is as a seed. It is small and it is weak but it can grow into something that is strong and mighty.'

That evening the earth oven was opened. The food that had been steaming in there for so many hours tasted delicious. There were pork and nuts and vegetables for everyone. The evening sun shone down on them even though the rain was falling on some of the hills around. It was a time of contentment.

Kepa had been watching, waiting for an opportunity to speak to this stranger, so different in his appearance, and yet talking their language. He could not really be a stranger. Making sure that Mondo was nearby, he crouched in front of Karl.

'My brother saved me from the fire,' he informed him. 'When he went to the hospital, I helped to look after him.' Karl was listening, seeing that the child was leading up to something.

'I wanted Mondo to go to the hospital so that they could put medicine in her eyes to make her see, but she was afraid.'

A laugh bubbled up from the blind girl.

'I am laughing because I am not afraid any more. Didn't the Lord Jesus hear me when I cried out to him when I was in danger? And didn't he lead me safely over the bridge, so that the other women had courage to cross? You said that the Lord Jesus could take the darkness of fear from my heart, and he is doing it.'

But then quietly she added, 'But oh, I would like to have light in my eyes so that I could read God's book.'

Karl sat quietly listening and praying. Then he leaned forward and spoke slowly.

'Mondo, we know that the Lord Jesus can open blind eyes. But sometimes he allows our disabilities to teach us other lessons. But if you and your people are willing, when we come back again from our country we will send for you.

'You can stay with us and we will give you good food and take you to the doctor. While you are with us my wife will teach you to read. We will ask to have a special book made in your language and she will teach you to read it by feeling the marks with your fingers.'

Mondo was gone. Moving from group to group she told them, 'I am going to read God's book. Jesus is going to help me to read God's book.'

Karl returned to where he had been sitting beside Kisoo. He reached out now and took the boy's hand in his. He held it very gently, twisted and scarred as it was.

'Do you know, Kisoo,' he mused, 'If your hands

had not been so badly hurt, you would no doubt have been taken away to work in the plantations. This has happened to so many of the young men.'

Kisoo nodded. He thought of his brothers, the boys that he had grown up with. Where were they now? Were they listening to God's word, walking in God's road?

'But God has given you a gift of teaching,' Karl went on, 'and I believe that he is going to use you to teach many people.'

'Tell him, Karl! Tell him!' interrupted Jon, who was sitting on the other side of the white man. His eyes were shining.

'Tell me what?' questioned Kisoo. What could there be that could make him happier than he already was?

'Why, when I come back from Australia we hope to open a Bible school, here in the highlands. I am going to speak to your village elders, because I want you to come to my school. You will learn more about God and he will use you to teach many people his word.'

'The rain is coming,' someone called and they stood up to go to their houses. As Kisoo walked with Karl and Jon he turned to see a beautiful rainbow spanning the valley.

'God's bow!' he whispered.

'Wasn't it through a bow that you first came to

meet Jon and to hear God's word?' asked Karl. 'Jon has told me.'

Kisoo hung his head. He was still ashamed of his foolishness.

'Yes, I had borrowed a stranger's bow and my brothers and I fought over it. When it broke I was so ashamed that I ran away.' And then he lifted his head. For had not very much good come out of this broken bow?

'And now God is setting his bow in the heavens to remind us of his word. His word is strong and true and his promises can never be broken,' declared Karl.

Kisoo's heart was full of joy as he went to the man house to sleep. Many wonderful things had already happened since the incident with the broken bow, and even better were still in store for him.